DECREPIT RITUAL

VALKYRIE LOUGHCREWE

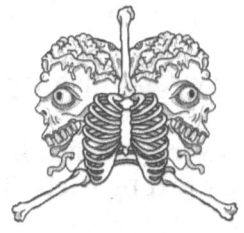

Ghoulish Books
San Antonio, Texas

Decrepit Ritual
Copyright © 2024 Valkyrie Loughcrewe

First Edition

All Rights Reserved

ISBN: 978-1-963801-04-0

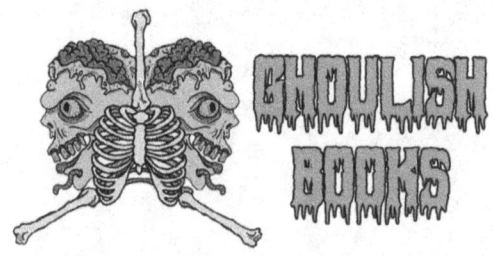

www.Ghoulish.rip

Front cover by Chris Maxwell
Front cover text by Zach Chapman

Also by Valkyrie Loughcrewe

Crom Cruach (2022)
To The Heart of The Dark (Anthology) (2023)
Spookshow (2024)

For Nanny,
Sweet dreams—and enjoy your garden

DRUNK AND HIGH as you are, you find yourself hesitating at the moment of suicide.

The bath is just about drawn, the painkillers have made everything numb, and the blade is waiting. New, out of the package, untainted by any previous cut. It's a fold-out black—handled straight razor. Giallo—style. Argento—style. You're going to find a little bit of flourish in the bleak mundanity of your final surrender.

You can't bear to look at the mirror, and you can't bear to strip off. You're not going to get into the bath all dressed up, so you're pacing. You step out into the living room of the cabin and you can't stop all these feelings. Tears are running down your face. You need to *stop* feeling.

This is what you came here for, isn't it? Out to this frozen middle of nowhere like the selfish piece of shit you are, to let the owner find your bled-out corpse when they realise that you never checked out? It's all too much, isn't it? Everything beyond the woods, the ceaseless noise, the endless profaning upon profanity. Man-made horrors beyond your comprehension, the teeth grinding dullness of watching the dignity being shaved off of everything, slice by transparent slice.

You're going through the bookshelves. Regular shit. Stephen King, Travelogs, Joyce, the novelisations of *Alien* and *Aliens* for some reason. You run your hand along the aged spines, and stop when you get to it. You know this book. You remember how your dad read it to you when you were a child, maybe once, maybe many times. You remember the laughter. He was quite the performer.

He'll miss you, and you don't care, do you?

No, it's far, far too much, having to care. Having to bear the weight of others.

You're on your knees now, going through the cupboards in the living room, the smell of the old carpet, saturated with years, generations maybe, of wood-smoke from the hearth, a pleasing sensation. You want to curl up and cry it out, get it all out so you'll be empty when you finally do it. Plenty of time. The ice in the tub won't melt here. The heat is off. No fire. The weather outside is literally Arctic.

Maybe you could just freeze yourself to death? That might be okay. It could be meditative, like one of those Buddhist monks who wall themselves off in a cave or get mummified alive.

Your body is going where it likes, your hands rifling through a cupboard, pulling out spare blankets, draping them over yourself. You find pillows, hug them close, make a little pile of them on the floor. There, at the bottom, you find homemade wooly socks ancient smelling, but clean. You put them on. The tears are coming again so you move to the next cupboard.

Small tools of different kinds—plumbing stuff mainly. Spare batteries. Boring. You consider throwing them all out on the floor, too, but loud metallic noises right now do not appeal to you. You don't want to make any sort of clatter or cacophony, you just want to fade away.

Under that, spare firewood—which you won't be needing. Save it for the next people who come to visit. Unless they close it down after finding your body. Maybe you'll haunt the place.

Being a ghost wouldn't be that bad, wandering the icy forests and tormenting the local Scandinavians. Hanging out with trolls. Even just to be that slightest noise—a rattling or banging—that someone would never ascertain was *Something* or not, now that would be to spit in the face of the dullness of forever.

Third cupboard, and two cylindrical objects fall out onto the pillow-strewn carpet with a soft rustling. They look like dark, glossy maps—no—posters? You look back into the cupboard. It's a single cubby, with another couple of those rolled-up whatever-they-ares and a cardboard box with—hot damn—film reels. Twin canisters peeking over the top of the box like skittish stray kittens.

Something throbs in you, through the painkiller haze, and you start to panic that the overdose might disintegrate your liver before you get a chance to investigate what you've discovered. Maybe you didn't take that many, and if it starts to hurt you can just get in that tub and slice yourself open.

And people say you didn't know how to relax!

You pull the box out of the cupboard. It's heavy, and you worry for a moment that you might drop it and spill the contents out onto the floor, but you keep it together and get it down onto the rug. There are four large canisters and several smaller, cylindrical ones. Are those for photo-film? You can't tell. This is Google's future, after all, and all that archaic shit is lost on you. You look down again at the fallen rolls, and you pick one up. White on one side, dark on the other, with writing and some kind of painted image.

You've found a goddamn movie poster.

Carefully you start to unroll it, not wanting to peek too early, so you take the top corner and tuck it under the bottom corner of the box of reels, the top right corner goes under a pillow, and fuck it, you guess that'll have to do for now, because you can't be fucked to move from this spot.

You roll it down. A painted fire, flames licking the top of the image. A fire in darkness, the orange-reds contrasting against edges of deep black. Rolling it down farther you see branches in silhouette—thin and disintegrating. A forest fire? Did they shoot a movie around here and forget to bring their reels back? You cannot possibly envision people doing something so stupid, but then again, people made NFTs of George Floyd, and other people bought them.

Fuck this world.

You almost let go of the poster as you see her face. Her eyes, her dark hair flowing as if in water. Her gaze pierces you, accusingly, and you feel dirty for having found her, stepping out of her inferno. You realise that you feel unworthy of seeing this face, bone-white flesh marred by spots of black rot—around the eyes, around the mouth, spidering across her cheeks, down over her chin, up across her forehead.

You laugh at yourself. You're pathetic, you know that? Ooh, you feel unworthy of looking at some painting? Some movie poster? Come on. You really don't have to beat yourself up over every little thing. But you can't fucking help yourself, can you?

Finish what you started.

No, no, not that. Not yet.

The poster.

Oh, right, yes, you're almost there now, you see more of her. Bare breasts covered by a spiked leather jacket, pretty much naked save for the jacket and what looks to be some kind of studded black leather cod-piece? Weird. Weird design. It deflates the image. That face that hit you so hard now looks, if anything, more pissed off about the fact that the poster artist drew her like this, profaned her. You're no prude or anything, but this just looks off somehow.

You finish unrolling the poster and that's it. This black metal chick walking through a forest fire, staring daggers at the viewer. She's holding a bloody bike-chain in one black-gloved hand and a long knife—the kind of blue-chrome, serrated knife-sword that only seems to exist in exploitation movie posters—in the other. There's no title, no tagline, nothing but that image.

You start to wonder if it might be some student project or something, part of some hipster art installation somewhere. Check out this corner of the warehouse, we have some old film reels and a poster of a character we designed halfway and then just decided fuck it—tits.

You sigh, letting the poster roll back up. You close your eyes, listening to the bath overflowing in the other room.

You should turn it off. You should get in, and let yourself leave this pathetic bullshit behind. Nobody ever does it right, nobody ever does what they're supposed to. Everyone lets the stupidest possible thoughts in their little monkey brains get in there, and fuck everything up.

"You deserved better," you croak through a numbed mouth.

Okay. It's time. It's time to go. Just stand up.

You do wonder what those film reels are stuffed with to make them so heavy. Might even be real film, like. That'd have been funny. If the whole art installation thing was to pull some film out of a canister and like, beat it up, expose it to light, drag it around. Give it the *Grindhouse* treatment. That would be fun. You reach into the box and pull out one of the reels, careful not to open it accidentally. If there is some lost indie flick on these you don't want to destroy it by accident. You can at least avoid ruining that before you go.

The canister has a scrap of ancient duct tape stuck to it, with *#1* written across it in black marker.

You set it down on the floor, unconsciously deciding that you're going to take these out one by one and stack them. You're delaying the inevitable, and knowing that makes you start to cry again. You reach to grab the second canister and notice something a little off. The depth of the box and the circumference of the canisters, the way they're tilting after you removed one of them. They're on top of something.

You pull the box closer, and look inside.

Your pulse spikes.

No way.

There's a black-spine VHS cassette box sitting underneath the reels.

There's a VHS player under the ancient CRT TV across the room for you.

Please don't be empty. Oh please don't be empty.

You take out the other canisters one by one, carefully.

You stack them on the floor, and you reach for the cassette case. Your hands are shaking. You lift it

It's got weight! There's a tape inside! A tape!

A movie! You're going to watch a movie! Won't that be nice?

A lovely movie in a lovely cabin! So, so nice!

The bath still overflowing, you scooch across the carpeted floor toward the TV. It's a tiny, grey thing, ugly as sin. There's a box for cable TV on a shelf above it, but you wonder why they even bother with that. Most TV is high-definition these days, probably wouldn't even fit on that tiny screen, and even still, most shows worth watching are only available on the unceasing miasma of endless streaming services.

Pointless. All so unbearably pointless.

Fuck this.

You kneel in front of the VHS player, cassette case in your hands. You haven't even taken the tape out yet and it's like, fuck this, you know?

You actually stand up for the first time in what feels like hours, and you turn around, walk back into the bathroom. The first thing you notice is your shiny new straight razor on the floor, water pouring over it. That's what you get for leaving it at the side of the overflowing bathtub. Great job!

The Carpet is soaked, and the water is spreading across the floor, soaking through your newly found homemade woolie socks.

Fuck this fuck this FUCK THIS.

You rip open the tape case and let it drop to the floor, falling facedown and swallowing up the razor from your view. The tape in your hands, to your surprise, has a label, and for a moment, your heart sinks. Through the blur of angry tears, that label could say anything. It could be *Barney the Dinosaur* for all you know. It could be a tape on maximising marketing potential for your ponzi scheme.

You're tempted to throw the tape into the bath, feeling

this horrible pull to chuck it in without even looking, to throw the thing in there and let it be fucking ruined and just slit your goddamn wrists over it and let your blood pour into it, let your blood wash away what could have been.

But you blink away the tears and you realise that the "label" is just another rectangular slice of white duct tape, and handwritten on it, in black marker, are two words:

DECREPIT RITUAL

There's a faint aptness there that takes you off guard for a moment. Your brain wants to wax lyrical on it as a moment of pure poetry—ah yes, this ritual, of suicide, in the uh, decrepitude of . . . society . . . but it fails to hang together in any transcendent way. Or maybe that's just you, never having been one to articulate your feelings very well. If figuring out what your place in all this was something you were good at, you wouldn't be here, would you?

But still, it did hit for a moment. It all made a kind of schizophrenic sense, and you can't deny that on an emotional level. It was nice to feel that. To feel like you had just stumbled across something meant to happen. You're putting too fine a point on it now, again. You can't just let moments be moments, can you?

God, you *are* grasping at straws, aren't you?

You tuck the tape under your arm and turn off the tap. You let the blade sit where it is, safe under the VHS case. But it's going to rust, isn't it? It won't be clean, won't be sharp enough to cut? Maybe bleeding out isn't the way you want to go. Maybe you do want to just take off all your clothes and walk out into the snow, and—

—no, no no no no! Commit, damn it! Commit to SOMETHING in your life for ONCE!

You step back out into the living room. Fuck fuck fuck fuck fuck. You need to go pick up the razor. You HAVE to do this. You HAVE to. You can't go back, it'll just be more suffering delaying a return to this moment. It's better to die out here than back there, than in the middle of all that misery and decay! Please!

Please, get away from the fucking VHS player—stop it. Stop it!

You push the tape into the slot and with a primordially satisfying series of clicks and whirs the tape is sucked into the machine. The screen bursts into static, the tracking info wavers on a blue screen. The play icon is there, the fuzz, the scanlines, all your friends are here in the one place! Isn't nostalgia fun? Welcome back to the womb, you pathetic fuck!

The image is silent for a moment, a shot of some bare trees under an overcast sky, looking through them, up toward the obscured glow of the sun. The trees are black, burned already. A trick of the light, maybe. An exposure issue in the camera. It all seems to throb with a multicoloured aura from the artifacting of the old tape, the player, the bad quality TV.

It almost looks like there's a human figure tacked up to one of the trees in the background, a withered corpse, like something out of the start of Herzog's *Nosferatu*, but the way it's all contrasted against the bleached sky you're not really sure what you're looking at.

A wind picks up outside the cabin, and you pull the blankets around yourself for warmth, for comfort. Then the music starts, a sustained synthesized pulse, cutting in mid-note as the tape audio catches up with what's being displayed.

There's a motorway slicing through the black woods, strewn with bodies, definitely, not just a trick of the light. Piles of white-shrouded corpses at the side of the road, which itself is cracked and overgrown. Where was this shot, you wonder? Soviet Russia?

You startle, as with a roar that crackles the TV's tinny speakers, a cherry-red convertible with the top down tears onto the screen, blasting down the ruined road as if it were the smoothest blacktop. It goes by too fast to get a look at the occupants, but its arrival heralds a John Carpenter bassline into the soundtrack. The car is a dot on the horizon in a moment, and the shot just lingers on the road for a little too long.

You're still wondering if this is some unfamiliar old exploitation movie or one of those modern retro-throwback things. It's hard to tell on this ancient screen.

The screen splits and distorts, great chasms of static boiling away the image. You worry for a moment that the tape might be damaged, but it ends up stabilising on a shot of fog enshrouding some dilapidated gas station. It really does look like some kind of war-torn Eastern European hellhole to you. The trees are all bare, everything is rusted and fallen into disuse. The store is ruined, glass broken, dust on everything. Out the front of the gas station, on an old rocking chair, lies another desiccated, skeletal corpse. It used to be wearing flannels, jeans and a sun hat, but the clothes are as decayed as the body itself.

This thing definitely has an atmosphere, but the tension of whether the tape is going to devour itself into snowy oblivion at any moment is bothering you somewhat. The movie can't end yet, although that would be fitting, wouldn't it? One last chance to connect with something other than yourself, denied.

The red car is back, rolling to a stop outside the gas station. It's pristine, positively shining in contrast to the crumbling grey-black bleakscape around it. You can see that from this distance, even with the pixellation of the CRT, but you still can't make out the occupants, and you know the movie knows it too, because the next shot is one of the character's boots as they hop over the side and bounce excitedly on the pavement. The laces are open, the boots unzipped over torn bleached denim jeans, and there are words painted in yellow on them. You only notice that last detail just before the shot cuts away, and your brain doesn't have time to register them.

SHIT FACE?

SLUT RACE?

Your brain isn't working as fast as it should be. It's the booze, the drugs. Those painkillers eroding the edges of your consciousness.

Another cut and there he is, throwing his arms wide. He's a full-on thrash metal guy, this black dude with no shirt on under his patch-covered denim jacket. He's not MCU-ripped, but the dude's in shape, and he's throwing his arms wide under the low hanging grey clouds and yelling.

"What a co-winkydink! We run out of gas, and there's a station right where we need it to be!"

He's manic, making big swings. Shades of Nicholas Cage, and he just stands there, vibrating and T-posing in front of the gas station as another thrasher, a white blonde chick with short, messy hair slides her arms around him, giggling.

And it cuts, and you gasp, and it's Her.

She emerges from the back seat, refusing to open the door as the other two did. Instead of a hop, though, she just steps over it like it's nothing. She is easily seven feet tall, if not just over, and she's built like a panzer. She's got the long dark hair, and what looks to be black metal corpse paint rotting into her flesh, but she's not topless like in the poster. Under the spiked leather jacket she's got on some band shirt with an indecipherable logo. Leather pants, huge combat boots, spiked black gloves. Another thing the poster didn't capture is that the actress has Asian features, whoever she is.

Seriously, though. who the hell *is* this giant musclebound woman? Why does she look like she's supposed to be undead or something? You barely have time to focus on her, as she just sort of walks away from everyone, offscreen, so you focus on the driver. Another woman, with close cropped springy hair, dressed in a tank top and camo pants, coloured the blue-greys of urban warfare (at least that's what videogames have told you those colours mean). She's black, her skin the kind of deep dark black you didn't really see cast in movies back then, whenever "then" is, and rarely even see in movies today (colourism is some deeply fucked shit). She steps out of the driver's side, using the door, clearly the first civilised person among her companions.

There's someone still left in the car. Someone in a black hoodie, shrouded in plumes of smoke. Weed? Cigar smoke? You're not sure. Did people wear hoodies in the 1970s-80s? They didn't, right? This *must* be modern.

There's a jarring cut, the footage threatening to disintegrate again, and suddenly the two thrashpunks are laughing like hyenas up on the front porch of the gas station. The girl grabs the jaw of that skeletal corpse on the porch, starts moving it around as she starts speaking a mocking kind of old man voice. The guy dips into the store, the old front door making that jingling sound that you only ever hear in movies.

"Ooh, you kids can't go down to the old cabin, it's got a death curse!" the thrasher chick imitates.

Is that a *Friday the 13th* reference? You look up to the cabin window, your vision swimming, and you feel a wave of nausea hit you. It's storming outside, a heavy, silent snow falling. You wonder how recently the cabin's previous occupants left. They had to be the filmmakers who worked on this, right? Maybe they are on their way back to the cabin right now to pick this stuff up, getting caught in the storm.

"Knock it off, you fuckin' neanderthals!" a man from the TV says. He doesn't sound like the thrasher guy. Maybe the hooded smoker?

You look back and see thrasher guy chuckling to himself, bursting out of the store, a rusted metal pipe in his hands as his girlfriend howls with laughter.

"Yer doomed!" she cackles. "Yer aaaaall doomed!"

Thrasher guy launches himself into frame and pulverizes the skeletal corpse with a swing of the pipe. It explodes into a cloud of dust, and the punks explode into raucous laughter. It cuts back to the guy in the car rolling his eyes. Yeah, that must have been the one who spoke, and that's definitely a blunt in his hand. His hoodie, at a closer look now, seems to be covered in subtle markings, the same colour as the rest of the jacket but glossier. They look like runes or something. Occult shit.

The image dissolves. Not into static, thankfully, but to a foggy clearing with a single, twisted, black tree in the centre of it. It has thorned-long, cruel bramble-thorns and there are bodies hanging from the branches, swaying on frayed nooses. Their ragged burial shrouds hang loose, as if the bodies are smaller than the ones you saw on the road. Dismembered, maybe, or the bodies of children, and She is there. The poster-girl, the undead metalhead giant, walking toward the tree slowly, reverently.

She places a spiked, gloved hand on the bark, stands level with a long, black thorn, and pushes into it, letting it pierce her between the eyes. It pushes deeper and deeper into her third eye point, drawing a thick bead of ruby red that rolls a rivulet down her bone-white nose.

And it's back to the parking lot. The thrashpunks are dancing, you think, your vision's starting to get hazy. There's thrash metal playing, maybe from a boom box? You can't fucking see!

Christ! These jump cuts are making your vision blur, and you're noticing your eye floaters, and that nausea that's been building isn't really going away. You close your eyes and grip your head and try to breathe through it. Fucking stupid body betraying you again. You should be allowed this ONE thing!

"Razor, Tank, we need to stay in character or this isn't going to work," the hoodie guy says.

"Stay in character? You fuckin' nerd," the thrashpunk guy (Razor? Tank?) is saying.

"Does this fuckin' place look like it's staying in character?"

DECREPIT RITUAL

You open your eyes, you see the soldier chick trying the pumps, but nothing is coming out. They're rusted so badly she's put down a can of kerosene she'd been carrying and is really having to squeeze them. She turns to the hoodie guy, who's still at the car, but is now sat up on the dash.

"*Does* it look like any of this is sticking to character, Acorah?" soldier chick says.

The hoodie guy, Acorah, sighs, and takes a frantic pull of his blunt, that delicious sucking-crackling-popping sound that makes you badly want a smoke. You could fish your tobacco out of your pocket but you know that you're too fucked up to roll. Acorah hops out of the car and walks toward the others with this weird, overly-exaggerated swagger, gesticulating wildly.

"Boy, am I glad we're all out here on SPRING BREAK!" He screams those last two words to the sky, throwing his arms back. Crows fly from the trees in the distant woods behind him.

"Time to get wasted, party down and go to town, am I right, Splatter?"

Sure enough, he says this as the undead woman melts out of the fog just in time for him to ensnare her into a bizarre, intricate series of high fives, fist bumps and other 'secret handshake' style movements. It's super dorky, and it ends just as suddenly as it began, and he moves on, leaving Splatter staring at her hand like she has no idea what just happened.

Splatter. God, what a name. You think you might be in love, and you're laughing—you're actually laughing because you're finding something funny for the first time in what feels like forever.

"Yeh-heahh, bring on the babes, bring on the beers, 'cause we are yooooung! Fresh meat baby, fresh meat!"

He's walking wide-legged now, a ridiculous looking gait, pointing at everything with finger guns. He takes the pump out of the soldier chick's hand.

"Here's to the best summer of our short lives," he says

with a wink, then squeezes the pump with ease. It spews gasoline out onto the concrete, and he hands it her, the smuggest look imaginable etched across his face. She arches an eyebrow.

"I will crush you, little man," the still-nameless soldier says, voice flat.

"I'd like to see you try," Acorah shoots back.

Tank and Razor stare at each other, open mouthed, and begin to chant before turning heel and racing back into the burnt-out store, excited as children.

"Beers! Beers! Beers! Beers! Beers! Beers! Beers!"

Splatter returns to the car, sitting in the middle seat of the back. Acorah clambers like a spider-monkey across to shotgun, and passes the boof to the goth giantess. She accepts it, blood still drying on her face, and takes a long drag.

"What did you see?" Acorah asks.

"Nothing," she replies on an exhaled cloud of smoke.

"Deader than dead. Listen."

A pause, she takes another drag. All that can be heard is the rumbling of the gas pump and the sound of the punks trashing the store.

"No birds singing," Splatter continues.

"No spirits howling out for sustenance. This place is old, depleted."

"Well that's what we're here for, I guess." Acorah says, shrugging.

The woman regards him with a look of puzzlement.

"What?" he asks. "You still think you came here to die?"

Your heart leaps a little, you almost expect his eyes to shift slightly, to look directly into the camera. Directly at you. No. You definitely came here to die. You're not doing anything special right now. You're just watching some weird arthouse metalhead hipster movie and—fuck. If you keep going, the painkillers are gonna wear off, and you'll have to go all the way into town and buy more and do this whole thing over again.

DECREPIT RITUAL

You should switch off the movie.

Come on, do it. Stop kidding yourself. It's time to go.

"Holy shit that actually worked! We don't have to drink fucking toilet gutrot tonight!"

The punk girl—it's gotta be Razor, right? Razor feels like a far more feminine name then Tank, doesn't it? She's falling back into the car with a crate of beer in her arms. Splatter steadies it, stops it from falling as she clambers into her seat.

"Babe," Tank says as he gets around to the door on the other side, hurt tinging his voice.

"I thought you liked my gutrot . . . "

"Oh I do, babe," Razor responds apologetically, sweet as a baby-doll.

"But you never clean that toilet."

Soldier-girl slams the trunk of the car, which apparently she had been rummaging in while you were having your little breakdown.

"Stow your shit and get in the damn car!" she barks, the militancy in her voice loud and clear.

Tank dumps his slab down in front of his seat, then hops the door, crouching over it like a goblin. He tears the top off of the crate and tosses a can to Razor, before popping one for himself. He looks back at Soldier Girl.

"Well what are you waiting for, Sasha? Let's go?"

Sasha! Okay! We're cooking now. Sasha rolls her eyes and takes her place as the driver. She goes to turn the key, and—

"Yo, one more thing!" Tank yells.

"Ugh, what?!!" Sasha groans, voice loaded with venom.

Tank hops out, rushes over to the dusty remains of the skeletal corpse, picks up the iron pipe and returns to the car. Sasha sits, glaring at him.

"Proceed," he says, sweetly as can be.

You're not laughing any more. Maybe the writing just isn't that good, or the acting is a bit stiff, or maybe you're just done. You are actually starting to like these characters, and it really isn't the acting. They're all pretty solid so far but you're just sort of feeling the novelty draining from this situation, and then Razor and Tank start singing, and you recognise the lyrics.

"Fall Break!" he yells, and non-diegetic synthpop music kicks in to match up with him.

"Fall Break!" Razor joins in, and they harmonise.

"Running in the sand, feelin' all right. And when you fall into my arms I'll break into your heart tonight . . . "

That's the fucking theme from *The Mutilator!* You know that one, you watched it on YouTube, what, must be almost ten years ago now? Weird. That movie has this bizarre, harsh proto industrial soundtrack, almost sounds like Nine Inch Nails at points, but then it has this totally cheesy theme song that's completely out of whack with the rest of the movie's tone, and now the characters in this flick are singing it as their red convertible zooms down the blasted, apocalyptic road?

It's *such* a weird fucking choice, that it just shuts off that voice inside you telling you to go back into the bathroom, back to pick up your razor, and you're so knocked off centre that the next thing that bursts onto the screen makes your jaw drop.

It's the cabin.

No, seriously, it's *The Cabin*. The one you're sitting in right now.

You had to be expecting that, right? After finding all this stuff here? But still, it completely throws you somehow, and that feeling you got from reading those words, DECREPIT RITUAL, from hearing Acorah say that line about coming here to die, it blooms in you, strong as anything, and you decide not to think about it this time, to just let yourself feel it, but even thinking *that* smothers the vibe completely.

Your stupid traitorous brain, always thinking, overthinking everything, dissecting every feeling like it's a frog tacked to a board. Why does your mind hate you *this* much?!

DECREPIT RITUAL

Even still, part of you wants to stand up and go to the window, like a kid at Christmastime waiting for Santa Claus, expecting that red convertible to carve its way through the snow, to pull up in front of the cabin and whisk you away to a new life inside the VHS player.

The clearing in which the cabin stands inside of the movie isn't even snow-covered, it's somehow dusty and swampy at the same time, and it seems to be covered in trash. The red car hasn't shown up yet, but you know that it's on its way. You're assailed with a series of images; dildos of various sizes hanging on a clothesline outside of the cabin, a stagnant paddling pool surrounded by a graveyard of empty liquor bottles. Cigarette butts, beer cans and the ends of spliffs choking the bare earth. It's a wasteland. The rotten core of the decaying forest.

This montage does little to ease your nausea.

The front door of the cabin, looking like it's covered in vomit, swings open. A pale, greasy man with long hair and a matted beard, naked save for shades, stumbles hangoveriously into the dim light. Through the door behind him red lights flash, shapes moving in the darkness—writhing—black latex—German Industrial/EBM blaring. He shuts the door as he staggers out, drunk and high out of his mind, dodging broken glass with filthy, fungus eaten feet.

It's me, you think, though you don't look much like the guy. He looks a lot like the way you really see yourself, if you're honest.

With a sigh of pleasure, the hideous man lets rip a forceful stream of red-brown piss against the ground about twenty feet away from the house, staring up into the cold blue-grey sky. He smiles—his teeth are bloody, and more blood trickles down from his nose. He's too lost in his medicated bliss to notice the blur of the red car coming around the bend behind him.

The nudity on display is pretty incredible, and how fucked this guy's body is, no offence but it's incredible that this guy allowed himself to go on camera like this. You didn't know it was possible to have a bush that thick.

The car is slowing to a stop, the tires sinking polluted sludge, and they're all doing the *Jurassic Park* thing, the punks are surfacing, standing up in their seats as the car slows. Acorah is standing too, Splatter joins the party. Only Sasha stays seated, staring daggers out through the windshield, at this ghoulish Pissing Man.

"Holy . . . " Tank says in an unflattering close-up.

"Fuckin . . . '" Razor snarls, a fish-eye lens right up her nose.

"Shit," Sasha grunts.

You're back over with Piss Man now, he's rolling his neck, jaw slack, dribbling blood. You can almost fucking smell him.

"Hey! You!" Acorah yells from the background.

The dude just keeps on pissing at full blast. Sasha reaches forward and cranks the radio. No response from The Urinator.

"Oh, fuck this douchebean!" Tank exclaims.

Tank ducks, comes back up with a can of beer that he throws in the air, catches it, and pitches it right at the Pissing Guy's head. The impact looks painful, but the dude just turns in slow motion, his stream of dark piss waning to a dribble before finally, mercifully ceasing.

A slow, anaesthetised grin spreads across his face as the scanlines begin to throb around him. His voice comes out corrupted by static.

"Oh, hey. New peep-par-party—new friends! Groovy!" He speaks in a cartoon surfer's drawl.

"How long have you been here?!" Acorah asks, breathlessly, looking shaken.

The naked man scratches his foul head.

"Oh, shit man, a long-ass weekend, couple a days, a thousand years, I dunno." He laughs.

"Who are you?"

"We're next in line, asshole." Sasha growls from the front seat.

"You're supposed to be dead," Splatter announces, loudly, clear as day.

"He just didn't show up!" Naked Guy responds.

Picture and sound start to decay. The sunglasses-wearing beard-freak is flapping his gums, clearly going on some kind of Manson-esque rant that you're finding it hard to make out through the fuzz, beyond the sight of his wild gesticulations. You're starting have faith, though, at this point, that the tape isn't going to fuck you over.

"—fuckin', drinkin', takin drugs man . . . gettin' freaky. The guy just never showed up, man!"

Tank and Razor share a wicked, grinning glance across the seats. They slide out of the car, on either side moving towards the naked man like wolves. Tank trails his iron pipe behind him in the sludge, and behind her back—your heart skips a beat—Razor flicks open a black-handled straight razor.

Don't think don't think just watch. Just feel it.

The naked guy doesn't seem to register the danger, and the video's starting to come apart more and more the closer they get to him. He's stammering, and—oh for the love of god—his dick is getting hard. This is definitely a European movie.

"Woah-hoh! You guys have some sick style, you know that? Come party, man, it's like a rave in there or somethin' and everybody is Dee Tee Eff—"

Sound and image snap back into full clarity as Tank drives the iron pipe with full force into the man's left knee. His frail limb bends backwards from the impact, and the jagged metal punches out the other end, spraying, splattering, pouring out thick dark blood.

The effect is glorious, John Carpenter's *The Thing* level of detail on the appliance combined with trick photography, it must be. The details on the leg are absolutely minute—right down to the leg hairs and the mole on the guy's shin!

Before the guy has the chance to scream, Tank shoves

the pipe through his other leg. Brutal! And these are supposed to be the good guys? The gore is offscreen this time, and you do hear a scream, a distorted woman's scream that strains the speakers on the TV. The shot cuts to fucking static again, but you think you can see the ghost of an image in the snow, repeated a few times and flickering across the screen. You scooch closer, and it gets clearer.

Yes, it's a woman—Jesus!—she's naked but for one of those novelty beer-hats and a strap-on, and she's standing in the doorway of the cabin, shrieking, red strobe light still going off in there behind her, filthy techno still blaring.

"Oh my GOD!" she shrieks. "HARRY!"

Razor growls, and spins, raising her namesake blade in a single fluid motion, and then runs full-tilt toward the cabin, holding her torso completely stiff with an eerie grin.

"Rachel!" Harry screams on broken knees, bleeding into the sludge.

"Get the gun! Get the—"

"Shut the fuck up!" Tank says cheerily, and just fucking smashes the guy's jaw off with the rusty pipe.

A child trying to blow out candles on a cake, huffing and puffing to the laughter and delighted gasps of your family.

Happy fifth birthday! Mommy and Daddy love you so very dearly! You can be anything you want to be!

A life of giggles and smiles awaits you!

The bearded, greasy man's blood leaking onto the poisoned soil, causing emerald blades of grass and pretty flowers to burst out of the muck in a time-lapse of growth. Tank just standing there pulverising his face through grunts of rage.

Happy birthday to you! Happy birthday to you!

Mutilated foam latex flesh bashed apart, plastic bone, corn syrup blood.

You're perched at the top of the stairs with a toy truck filled with dolls, your mother is younger than you are now, she's ready to hold you back if something goes wrong. You giggle and screech as you roll the truck toward the edge of the top step and—

You're staring at the ceiling of the cabin. You're flat on your back and you're paralysed. The wind is rattling the windows and your head is spinning, and before you know it you're sputtering out gobs of thick puke out all over your face—it fills your mouth, it backs up into your throat. It gets in your eyes and you're choking but you can't move. Flailing phantom limbs, you feel your body sitting up a thousand times but your flesh doesn't follow suit.

Oh god, is this it? Choking to death on puke as distorted synth-bass tries its best to pump out of a shitty TV set in the middle of nowhere, Norway?

You don't wanna go, not yet. Not like this.

Sasha's standing around the back of the car again, popping the trunk. Steadicam moves in, like a Michael Myers POV shot to show you what she's gone back there for. It's neatly arranged in indentations in the material, like a gun case. Armour. Some kind of futuristic pistol, the kinda chunky Robocop-looking gun kids bought one-dollar replicas of at gas stations, with SPACE POLICE written on the box, and pieces of what must be another weapon, disassembled.

She pulls out what looks like a metallic black beetle and places it on the back of her head, which immediately begins to build out into a jet black Tokusatsu-looking helmet. The effect is stop-motion, miniature superimposed over the actress's face. Has there even been any CGI so far? If there has, you haven't noticed.

As the helmet encloses around her face, she starts assembling that other weapon.

"Move away from the cabin, children!" she chides, her voice amplified by the helmet.

You always hated hearing your voice in these home movies, even as a kid. You wonder who it was who taught you to hate yourself, if anyone. Maybe you were just built for it, factory-designed to self-destruct.

Razor bangs her fists against the vomit-encrusted front door of the cabin. Her namesake is already implausibly buried into the door like an axe. You must have missed that part when you were—

—while you were—

—Tank grabs Razor away from the door, pulling her to the side as a shotgun blast busts a hole in it from within.

"Move it, you crazy bitch!" he yells.

"I!!!" Razor begins.

"Want!!!" she continues.

"BLOOD!" she howls, as Tank brings her down to the ground, and plants a sweet little kiss on the end of her nose.

"Well you're about to get a flood of it, baby," he coos.

Blood leaking from chasmous mutilations, pouring, feeding the soil, giving rise to fresh greenery. Cigarette butts and broken glass dissolve as flowers bloom in their stead. Splatter cracking her neck in the middle of it all, Sasha stepping up beside her, raising a high-tech rifle right out of a graphics card commercial, that seems to be interfacing with her helmet, from all the blinking blue lights and futuristic blooping.

"Swiss Cheese and Voorhees?" Sasha says, her voice modulated beneath the helm.

"Sounds good to me," Splatter replies, and walks out of sight.

Tank and Razor scramble away from the Cabin when they hear Sasha's weapon begin to emit a building mechanical whine, the kind that never tends to herald anything pleasant. She flicks a switch near the stock of the rifle, the blue lights turn red.

"Ho ho ho," she deadpans, and all hell breaks loose.

The weapon unleashes a high-powered torrent of death on the wooden facade of the cabin, firing with the speed and intensity of a minigun. Windows shatter, the door is left a perforated pulp. As the rifle cools down, the cabin is left indeed looking much like swiss cheese.

DECREPIT RITUAL

It really looks like they shredded the shit out of this place with something, maybe an actual rifle, maybe a shitload of squibs. Must have cost a fortune to rebuild to the state it's in now. So there's no way this thing was filmed any time recently.

"How much ammo you got in that thing?" Tank asks, bopping into frame with Razor in his arms.

"It's best not to think about it too hard," Sasha responds.

You're with Splatter again, sneaking around the side of the cabin, machete drawn. It's not the absurd giant serrated combat knife of the poster, just your average everyday machete. No sense in messing with a classic.

Oh! There's the back hall with the bedrooms and the bathroom, adjoining the living room which you're sitting in right now. In the movie, the German EBM is still blaring from here through the closed hall doors. Splatter climbs in through the window and you swear to god the pipes in here just clacked as her boots touched the floorboards in the movie. Definitely the pipes. Although, didn't you have the heating off?

Light streams through holes in the south and north facing walls where Sasha's gunfire tore through the hallway, but aside from that, the hallway is dark. The soundtrack is silent save for the creaking wood and the sound of a man crying, which fades out of the relative silence and sends the hairs on the back of your neck rising. You shift uncomfortably, and your hand touches something cold and mushy.

You recoil, looking down to see puke. At some point you must have vomited, and there's a LOT of it. The remnants of your Last Meal On Earth is spattered across the rug. The camembert, the seafood, the mushed-up burger and chicken. You feel no small measure of shame reneging on your vegetarianism on your way out.

You start to remember choking on your own puke, being unable to sit up. How did you get out of that? And why don't you remember? Adrenaline maybe? You want to move around a bit more, maybe to clean, but your body feels so heavy, and Splatter is moving silently as a ghost towards the door where the sound of the crying is coming from. She closes her eyes, takes a deep breath, and shoves her machete through the lower half of the door. The blade cuts through the wood like it's butter, the crying becomes a ragged death-rattle, blood seeping down out of where the machete pierced the door.

Splatter turns around to see the Blonde from earlier tiptoeing backwards around the corner, shaking and gripping a shotgun. The woman, Rachel, lit by a shaft of pulsing red light from the now-open door to the living room, seems to be oblivious to Splatter's presence. She falls backward, pressing her back against the wall, and slides down to the floor. A blood trail follows her down the wall—she's been shot.

You watch Splatter creep towards her, eyes shining like a dog's in the darkness, pale face made all the more daemonic by the high contrast red pulse of the strobe. Rachel notices her far too late. She whips the gun towards Splatter, who kicks it out of the way as it goes off. The sound of the gun drowns out all noise and leaves both Splatter and the woman's ears ringing.

Splatter delivers a heavy boot to the woman's head, before leaning her full weight into her skull. The woman's head erupts, brains spurting out from splitting bone, the thick mush borne on a tide of blood, blackened by the crimson strobe. A shudder runs through the leatherclad murder machine, and she lets loose a ragged sigh.

The strobe goes out again, leaving you in the grainy-multicoloured darkness of the CRT screen, your face reflected back at you. You wince at the sight of yourself, pale and stained and medicated, your eyes bloodshot, only half open. The red light returns, and it's just like watching the reflection of yourself and the room morph into another version of itself. Instead of a cozy holiday home, it's shredded bacchanal, all bright red horrors and deep sinister shadows. Instead of your obscene visage staring out, a dark figure hangs suspended from hooked chains, its body encased in PVC. The figure is swaying softly, pouring blood like a showerhead after having been perforated by Sasha's ranged assault on the cabin.

You can just about make out three other bodies in the pulsating gloom. One man dressed in leather dom gear, one woman tied up in bondage and one guy splayed on the couch in a Hawaiian shirt, and nothing else. Splatter melds out of the black static, prowling like a cat. She steps toward the hanging body, and—with a grunt—decapitates it with a single stroke of her machete. She stands before the rush of blood, letting it wash over her face.

The strobe goes out, the music along with it, and you're left alone again with yourself.

"Ho ho ho," you mumble, before bursting into laughter.

Your chest hurts, oh God, the laughter knocks the wind out of you.

"That's brought some life back into this place, huh?" Razor's voice, from the TV.

You look up, startled. This movie is fucking with you, right? It's got to be. On screen, Razor, Tank, Sasha and Acorah stand out front of the cabin. The greenery is spreading, and even some trees are starting to grow around them. The effects work is mind-boggling, you're trying to figure out how it was done. It has to be some kind of green screen, CGI-type shit, right?

It reminds you of the trick photography that *Game of Thrones* used to create its giants, and giant wolves, and wall-crawling zombies. How it just sort of casually dropped some of the best effects work you've ever seen in front of you and left you wondering how it was done.

"Hey, does that mean we're all gonna be butchered tonight?" Tank asks. His tone is weird, it's salacious somehow. Flirtatious even.

He looks over to Acorah, who shrugs, lighting up another blunt.

"Clear!" Splatter's voice rings out from inside the cabin.

A jump cut. Tank's now drinking out of a large plastic bottle of a foul-looking liquid, with GUTROT written on it in marker, as he stares at the headless gimp chained to the ceiling

"I guess this is what happens when you try to keep a party going inside a horror movie. Things get dark," he opines.

The living room is lit properly now, and the extent of the filth of the room, even from just what you can see from this angle, is atrocious. Piles of trash, rotten food everywhere. A lot was hiding in those stark shadows created by the red strobe.

"Don't kinkshame," Razor chides her partner.

Acorah pulls the mask off of the dead gimp—the face underneath is heavily scarred, the lips, eyelids and nose cut away.

"This is beyond kink, man," he says. "This is getting into some Italian knockoff of *Hellraiser* shit."

"So what are we gonna do?" Tank asks. "Clean up these assholes' fucking mess? I just wanna get fucked up and wait for the rumble!"

Sasha stands pensively by the window, heavy curtains pulled apart to let in the sunlight. She glances from the window to the group, no light reflecting off her vantablack helm.

"Hey, Splatter?" she asks softly. "Could, you, uh—"

Splatter nods, grabs two of the chains, and with a single yank of her muscular arms—rips the corpse down onto the ground. The group around her flinches, as if expecting the roof to come down with them, but it's a clean rip, and one chain is left hanging, adorned with a scrap of glistening flesh and leather.

The two-tone giant plucks this remaining gore from the hook, and without a moment of hesitation, drives the hook into her third-eye point. She grimaces. The thrashpunks cheer her on, grinning like lunatics.

"The forest is waking up," she begins, eyes rolling back in her head. " . . . Rejuvenating . . . the spirits of gore and death are . . . something's emerging, forming. It's going to be new, and hungry and eager to impress."

Sasha exhales loudly, the helmet's modulation making the sound come out oddly musical.

"Impress, huh?" Razor sneers. "Sounds like corpse monger speak for no fucking mercy."

Tank shrugs, raising his stained tub of gutrot.

"I say fuck it!" he declares. "We die, we feed the woods, everything's just the way it should be, and we go on to the next life. So let's eat, drink and be merry, baby!"

Sasha's helmet visor opens. She's staring into space, looking like the next words she's about to say are eating their way out of her against her will.

"I say we burn this fucking cabin to the ground."

Acorah's eyes widen. "Yes!"

Now there's an idea, you think. If these painkillers are actually gonna waste you, why not leave a little havoc in your wake? Set a fire, let the place burn to ashes around you as you die. You become aware that you've been idly, slowly arranging the pillows around you to prop up your increasingly paralytic body. Keeping your head elevated, face pointed toward the TV at a good-enough angle. It's an incredibly unnatural shape for your body to be in, and you'd probably be aching if you could feel anything.

"Break the ritual entirely?" Splatter asks. "What will that accomplish?"

You consider moving. You might be doing serious damage to your spine right now. Fuck knows you don't want to come out of this thing crippled for life, although that being said if you do end up unable to move, you'll just freeze or starve. You should have just taken the razor when you had the chance.

"It'll send a message," Sasha says. "We're not your

average college kids on the butcher's block. We're steppin' up the game."

Acorah looks like he can barely contain his joy. He's squirming, positively vibrating. The image seems to be distorting around him, but that just could be your eyesight deteriorating. Tank looks less enthused.

"Uuugh, and then what?" Tank groans. " Run around in the woods in the dark and get killed by fuckin' mud men, or zombies, or werewolves or some shit? That sounds lame as fuck. At least in here we got booze and a fire!"

"So then we bulldoze the fuckin' woods, Tank," Razor exclaims. "I'm with Sasha! We got a unique opportunity here. You hear me, God?! Give us somethin' new!"

Splatter's face swims in front of your eyes, the natural light and shadow highlighting the sheer corruption of her flesh. You find yourself wondering if the actress is that beautiful without the makeup appliance, or if it's the corruption that makes her as striking as she is.

"I must be clear with you all," she says. "As a Corpse Monger, the most logical thing for me to do would be to kill every single one of you. Which I could do rather easily, and then take the place as the new slasher in this place. That seems, almost overwhelmingly, like what I was built to do. However, I am very aware that this is a unique opportunity and that we could potentially move on to bigger and better things if we stick together."

"Christ, Splatter, thank you for candour," Tank scoffs. "Remind me not to let you outta my sight."

"You would be my first kill," Splatter says, deadpan.

"No offense, guys," Acorah says with a loud clap. "But, do we not think that we might be a tad under-equipped to take on the great unknown? I mean, Sasha, you've got your Darkshock shit, Tank's got his pipe which . . . could suffice, and Splatter is . . . a fucking Corpse Monger but I got nothin' but magic and it's not like I can cast fuckin' lightning bolt, know what I'm saying, and Razor, no offence I know it's your name but I don't think a straight razor is gonna, y'know, cut it if shit gets real."

"Hey, fucko!" Razor hisses, pointing with her weapon. "A straight razor is a fucking iconic weapon. I bet you a dick in the ass that I could slice you in the neck with this shit and it would be like you never had any goddamn bones in your body. Head would come right off!"

"Look, that's all well and good if you're murdering fucking Opera singers but that thing's about good for one hit to the eye of a slasher and then what, your fists? Come on now." Acorah grins like a shark.

"Acorah, stop bitching, okay?" Sasha says, exasperated. "You wanna stock up? Stock the fuck up—you're a wizard, aren't ya? Make that shit happen. I'm going to get suited up outside. Unless you wanna use my sidearm?"

Acorah shakes his head.

"Nonono. No. I think too much. I'd run outta ammo."

Sasha clomps out of the room and Acorah starts pacing.

"Ooh, is it magic time?" Razor asks mockingly.

Acorah looks frustrated, he's groaning, stimming. He stops, framed with the others watching over his shoulder, and he does that thing where he runs his hand across his face, wiping his expression from one of profound frustration and stress to one of wide-eyed wonderment. He spins on his heel back around to face his comrades.

"You guys hear about the old man who used to own this cabin? Doctor . . . I dunno . . . Ed . . . Scary?"

Razor snorts with laughter. Acorah's expression strains.

"Yes, I've heard of him," Splatter says, motioning Acorah to continue.

"Okay, great!" Acorah says, rolling with the energy. "Legend has it he was this, like, mad doctor, who kept himself alive by sewing still-living parts of his victims onto himself, right?"

Acorah steps backwards, floorboards creaking under

his sneakers. He's moving toward a bookshelf. It seems bizarrely clean and bright compared to the rest of the party-soiled dungeon that the cabin has become within the movie, and you realise as he gets closer that it is the exact same bookshelf that's on the wall off to your right. You turn your head over to see and yeah. Same arrangement of books and everything.

Right? You look back at the movie, back at the shelf, and you're making yourself want to throw up again, but neither of them change. It's the same. Even that fucking book Dad used to read to you. That's weird, right? That's . . . something?

"They say he has a full medieval lab under this place, filled with torture devices, medieval weaponry of all kinds, just like new, and some say, locked down behind thick, inescapable iron bars—"

The wizard in black reaches out for the shelf, his hand tracing across the spines of the books—King, travelogues, Joyce—stops at The Book. Your book, and he pulls it, and that stupid pathetic insane part of you that you've beaten down every moment of your life expects the book on the shelf across from you to fall, but all that happens is that the one in the movie starts to move. It slides open, revealing a secret passageway. A stone staircase, lit by torches, real medieval shit.

"The cries of his old experiments can still be heard," Acorah finishes, a trembling in his voice.

He turns to face his captive audience. They look thoroughly unimpressed.

"Medieval Weaponry?" Tank asks, eyebrow arched.

"Swords don't run out of ammo," Acorah says, turning to head down the staircase. "Come on."

"Oh, I'm not going down there, dude," Razor says.

"What, are we splitting up now?" Tank scoffs. "Super smart idea, Acorah! Real big brain shit."

"Oh my God, relax! The old man who owned this cabin is Part 4 in space by now, or maybe even terrorising Manhattan. We're good. C'mon."

They shake their heads at him.

"No fuckin' way," Tank says, grinning apologetically.

Acorah pinches the bridge of his nose. The cut to outside the cabin hurts your eyes. It's brighter out now. Greener. The sky a chromatic blue-orange as the sun starts to set below the dispersing clouds. Sasha is there, in the middle of donning her suit of black, plated armour. Acorah sticks his head out the window of the cabin.

"Hey Sash!" he yells. "The punks won't come into my magical murder basement and I need backup."

"Can I finish getting dressed first?" she calls back, screwing the helmet into the armour's spine.

You watch it fold into the body armour like living origami, and then she's walking down those stone steps beneath the cabin, assault rifle in her grip but helmet faceplate open. She moves like a SWAT team pointman. Acorah follows behind, for once not trailed by a constant cloud of smoke. He looks uncertain, fidgety, hands unable to stray far from his pockets.

"Okay," he mutters under his breath as they reach the bottom of the stairs.

A great wooden door awaits them, something straight out of a *Dungeons & Dragons* manual from the 80s. Massive metal ring pull and everything.

"Presenting . . . the armoury!" Acorah says, reaching out to pull the door open.

A sterile white light pollutes the medieval atmosphere. Sasha keeps her gun trained on the door as Acorah heaves the door open to reveal a white-walled hospital corridor. Dark wards lie behind mesh-enforced glass, empty gurneys lie in the hallway.

"A hospital?" Sasha asks. "Where are you gonna find a sword in a—"

A PA system in the corridor screams to life, and you feel a shock run through your body. The noisy jumpscare was cheap, but your head is suddenly a lot clearer than it was. You take advantage of this brief adrenaline burst and crawl up onto the couch. It's not that much more comfortable than the floor, to your disappointment.

"Greetings. My name is Doctor Edward Scary—" a low-pitched, gloopy voice says over the PA. "It is time to indulge in a little medical experimentation."

"Fucking. Run," Acorah says.

You hear heavy boots on stone, and turn back to face the screen just in time to see Acorah and Sasha have steel, elevator-style doors shut in their faces as they reach the top of the steps, cutting them off from the cabin.

Razor and Tank rush over to the steel doors. Tank tries to jam his iron pipe in but he can't fit it into the crack. Razor turns to Splatter, who is standing at the window, looking away from them, worry on her face. She's watching the greenery outside, the birds flying, the trees that are still growing because of their bloodshed.

"Splatter!" Razor yells, eyes wild. "Get yer dead ass over here and help us!"

Pale hands scrabble against the dark windows of the hospital wards. Gurneys are pushed out of the way as a horde of nightmarish figures begin to pour into that hospital corridor. Doctors and nurses wielding rusted surgical tools, patients in straitjackets, shot through with metal implants—all of them with masses of twitching scar tissue in place of faces.

"Your handlers are coming to collect you now," the voice on the PA says, sounding less and less human by the syllable. "It shouldn't take long."

Sasha is trying to punch her armoured fingers into the gap in the steel door, making the tiniest gap. Tank is managing to wedge his pipe in the slightest fraction, but cannot get the door to budge farther.

"But . . . if they die, it will feed the world. It would be good," Splatter says, quietly, staring at the sky.

The creatures are getting close now, their shadows visible around the corner of the downward staircase. Acorah is gripped with terror, hanging on to Sasha.

"Sasha!" he screams.

"Fuck!" she yells, breaking away from the door, shutting closed what little give she'd eked from it.

She spins, helmet closing over her face, and the first of the horrors round the corner. Sasha unloads a stream of white-hot bullets into the mutants, tearing through flesh, exposing subdermal mesh, metal bones. There's not much in terms of impact-splatter or blood spray, it's more like a power washer stripping away the layers until it punches right through, leaving ragged chasms of dripping black ichor.

Each ghoul is managing to make a frightening amount of distance before falling, just within swinging distance, within grabbing distance, replaced immediately by another, and another. Sasha screams as she fires, barely dodging out of the swipe of a metallic claw which rakes a deep gouge into her armour, sparks spraying like arterial blood.

"Fuck Fuck Fuck FUCK!" Acorah pulls a swiss army knife out of his pocket and cuts into his arm—then hastily paints some kind of rune onto the door in his blood.

Razor breaks away from the door, runs up on Splatter and punches her in the face. Splatter is barely fazed, but she does snap her gaze on Razor, eyes wide, mouth slack, as if just being woken from a trance. Razor staggers backwards, gripping her aching hand.

"Stop thinking with your fucking machete, you pissant Corpse Monger!" Razor yells, cringing from the pain.

Splatter shakes her head, snarls, and rushes towards the door, smashing her fingers into the gap between the doors and starting to wrench them apart. She's exerting all of her strength, screaming in rage as her muscles strain, but you see what they're trying to show you. Splatter is one strong piece of work.

Acorah wriggles through, and scrambles as far away from the door as possible. Sasha steps back through the door, firing. One patient-mutant lurches forward through the door, shredded up by gunfire but still moving. Splatter steps back and lets the doors close with a *shunk*—slicing the ghoul clean in half. Without missing a beat, the severed torso continues crawling, its gnarled fingers scrabbling against the stained floorboards, fingernails breaking away, stuck on by strands of yellowish gunk.

The thing's making a beeline towards Acorah, who looks paralysed with fear, prone on the ground, until Splatter brings a foot down onto its back, and pins it. Sasha levels the rifle to the shuddering discoloured mass of its head. Her helmet folds back into the body of her armour.

"Handle this, motherfucker," she spits, before blasting the creature's face into a blackish-purplish pulp.

As the sound of the gunshot fades, all that can be heard is Acorah laughing his ass off. The laughter infects Sasha and she breaks down too.

"Did you just?! Fuckin' say?! HANDLE THIS?! Oh man, that was fuckin' classic!" Acorah howls.

Sasha pops open a compartment on her thigh-armour, and pulls out a floppy-disk-sized object that unfolds into that gas station toy looking handgun. She hands it down to Acorah.

"Better than nothin'," she says. "Use a mantra or something."

"Soooo . . . " Razor says inquisitively. "You guys wanna burn this place to the ground?"

Splatter sighs heavily.

"Yeah," she groans. "Why not."

The sudden crash-zoom of Tank screaming and pouring a beer over his head takes you off guard, and another wave of laughter pulses out from the inside of your chest.

"LET'S PAAAARTYYYYYY!" the thrasher screams, launching his boombox down onto the floor of the cabin.

The soundtrack erupts into some gnarly cover of .45 Grave's "Partytime", and your senses are assailed by a quick-cut montage. You can't quite make out through the guttural vocals if they're using the lyrics from the *Return of the Living Dead* version of the song or the original lyrics about a little girl getting molested at her fourth birthday party. You really, really hope it's the former. You like your art edgy but not *that* edgy.

Tank is pissing on a rug. They're tearing down doors and smashing what windows have yet to be smashed, ripping banisters off of the staircase. There's a brief shot of Razor and Tank having a dildo fight. Splatter piles all the corpses into a mass just out front of the cabin as the others are making a bonfire of broken furniture in the living room.

You watch Splatter ripping the corpses apart, scattering the gore like confetti, stomping them into mincemeat. Brambles grow out of the pile of bodies as she artfully mutilates them. Beautiful flowers blossom on the thorny vines to the sound of a shrieking guitar.

The sound breaks off, flickering, echoing, as Razor's face swims into focus, her eyes wide. She's upstairs, walking towards something you can't see. She's half lit from below the stairs, motes of dust drifting peacefully around her. The object of her focus turns out to be a strange looking door, carved out of a solid-looking green wood. It seems to be carved with a design of thousands of caterpillars eating each other—a chaotic maelstrom of cannibalistic pupae.

The door is, as far as you're aware, the main bedroom, where your unpacked backpack is lying right now just above you. Razor's mouth scrunches up into a self-consciously punk sneer, she lashes out a kick with her unlaced boot, and it swings open in a cloud of—fog? Smoke?

No, incense. The room is full of these incense sticks all over the floor, in a ring around this . . . what is that, some kind of floating figure? You can't quite make it out through the wafting clouds and decrepit VHS quality footage, but around it there are these bundles of alien-looking herbs hanging dried and tied together from the beans, and there's sigils drawn and scratched into the walls in fibonacci spirals in chalk.

Yeah, there it is in a closer shot. A small figure, about the size of a teenage girl, floating on its back, limbs dangling, head back, wearing thick sackcloth robes.

"What the fuck?" Razor says under her breath.

She steps forward, getting a better look at the entity's face through the haze. It's pale, greenish, and femme, and it's got three eyes, all rolled back up into their cavities. The eyes are black, and beady, like the eyes of birds. Its translucent eyelids are fluttering, deep in REM sleep.

Razor starts slowly circumnavigating the floating anomaly, entranced by its weirdness.

"Hey Razor, you looking to get cooked alive up there?" Tank calls up from the bottom of the stairs.

"You—" She tries to respond, but her voice comes out cracked. "You guys should—!"

The robed figure shrieks, its voice crowlike, piercing, and it falls to the floor with a textile flump. It starts to convulse, foaming at the mouth, blacks of its eyes rolling back, giving way to wild, staring human eyes, the third eye squeezing shut. It spasms, choking on the foam erupting from its spluttering mouth.

"Oh shit, Oh my God!" Razor is stammering.

She's kneeling toward the convulsing figure, holding her gloved hands out in a gesture that indicates she's unsure of whether she wants to help the thing or keep it at a distance. Neither of these approaches work out, as a skinny fist flies out from the mass of shifting fabric and socks her one, knocking her back onto her denim clad posterior.

Razor seems stunned enough by the punch to let the thing scramble away out the door. It's unnervingly fast, moving in that weird frame-chopped Grudge Girl way.

It rushes out onto the landing, right into Sasha, Sasha startles, yelling something in fright. It sounds to you like she said, *"I knew it!"* Her training kicks in as a shock response—instead of flinching she snaps her rifle sights on the thing in an instant.

The pale figure shrieks again, and it throws out a pale, slender hand as if it was batting away a fly. Sasha's aim veers off in the direction of the swipe the split second before she fires, the burst drilling a hole in the wall, firing through into the master bedroom and—Oh fuck!—blowing Razor's left leg off at the knee in a crunchy balloon-burst of gore!

The shock of having her aim thrown off causes Sasha to lose just enough composure to give the pale humanoid a chance to skitter past her and onto the stairs, where it meets Tank, screaming and charging with his pipe.

The thing chooses that moment to leap off the staircase, right out of its robes, and perch naked and pale on Tank's shoulders. Six insectile wings blast open with a splattery flourish of clear fluid, and the humanoid leapfrogs Tank, gliding toward the door just as Acorah steps into the threshold.

Shit goes full *dreamweaver* for a second as Acorah sees the dragonfly-winged, three-eyed, naked pixie thing flying towards him, full vaseline on the lens slow motion with warpy synth music, before it all snaps back and he sidesteps the thing, letting it out of the house.

"Holy shit," he says to himself, before running out of the house in pursuit of the anomaly.

He doesn't have to run far. The thing's flown right into Splatter's grasp, her studded, gloved hand tightly clutching its throat.

There's a brief moment of silence, filled a moment later by the sound of Razor screaming in pain. Tank calls her name as he rushes up the steps to her aid. Sasha lingers at the top of the staircase for a moment, before opting to abandon the punks.

The sun is really setting now, and framed before the tangerine haze of the dying light over the withered blackened trees, the pixie-thing is struggling against Splatter's one-handed chokehold. The hulking death-metal giant lifts the anomaly's face to her own.

"Hello, little thing," she purrs.

"Stop!" Acorah yells. "We need to know what it is!"

"It's meat," Splatter chuckles, reaching for her machete.

The humanoid's third eye opens. The three eyes roll back to black. Splatter tilts her head slightly, curious for a moment, and a rivulet of blood trickles out from her right nostril. Splatter's grip loosens so violently you hear her knuckles snap, and she drops to the ground convulsing.

The anomaly takes off like a shot, running through the freshly grown grass toward the woods, building momentum, wings flitting in preparation to launch itself over the tree-tops. The wind blows its greasy, weedlike hair and an expression of bliss spreads across its uncanny face. Acorah races after it, arms and legs pumping. Sasha emerges from the house and kneels by Splatter in the background.

She's yelling something, but she's too far away for you or the wizard to make it out.

Acorah stops dead as the anomaly takes flight, making quick distance over the treetops. The wizard grits his teeth, and—eyes glazing over—he pulls out Sasha's pistol. He aims it with both hands before letting loose a quick barrage of shots. The pistol barely bucks but bellows out railgun lines of white hot ejecta.

One of the shots connects, and the distant figure plummets like a downed chopper in a flutter of shredded wings. Acorah starts to come out of his glazed-over expression, and begins to tremble. He looks down horrified at the weapon, breaths coming sharp, shallow and sudden.

Splatter's going into spasms, vomiting up a stream of brown sludge, infested with wriggling worms and maggots. Sasha is clearly panicking, trying to get Splatter to stop contorting.

DECREPIT RITUAL

Razor screams through a mouthful of torn denim, as Tank pours his gutrot over her stump, shirtless now, having given Razor his battle jacket to bite down on. He pulls out a cheap plastic lighter from his pocket and sparks it.

"This is gonna hurt!" he yells, and Razor screams again.

Splatter is flat on her back, hemorrhaging dark brown slime, blood and worms, out of her mouth, nose, and now eyes. Her skin is getting even more decayed. She's making hideous gurgling sounds. Sasha puts her rifle up to Splatter's face. Splatter meekly gropes at the barrel—and you're not quite certain if she's trying to stop Sasha or steadying her aim.

"I'm so sorry," Sasha says, looking genuinely distraught.

"Don't!" Acorah yells, skidding to a stop in the grass beside Splatter.

He fishes into the pockets of his hoodie and pulls out what looks to be some kind of white-handled ritual dagger.

"I can cut it out of her," he says, lifting it to the bleary orange sky.

The sunlight glints off of a metallic Eye-In-The-Pyramid set in the hilt, and Acorah cries out to the forest all who may watch from within and beyond it.

"LEVIATHAN! CHORONZON! AHRIMAN!"

He plunges the blade into Splatter's belly. He takes a breath, and then rips the blade down her abdomen, creating a tear and releasing a cloud of flies into his face. The wound begins to leak, a thick mass of what looks like wormy, bloody shit. Acorah drops the dagger and plunges his hands into the gruesome molasses.

What he pulls out is hideous to the point of making you briefly consider looking away. At first a bunch of thickly flaccid, unpleasantly glistening flesh. As it comes spurting out into the dusklight it starts to look like a cross between a whelk and an octopus, a coral-like shell perforated with squirming snails' heads at the end of long tentacle-like appendages.

Tank and Razor emerge from the darkness of the cabin, furious, Razor hanging off of Tank to avoid falling over. She looks barely conscious.

"SASHA, YOU MOTHERFUCK—!" Tank starts to rant, waving his pipe like an angry old man with a cane.

Sasha looks back at him, her expression hard, her face tear-streaked. Acorah turns too, his expression manic.

"Tank! Batter up!" he cries out, and throws the squirming abomination right at him.

Tank reacts quickly to the hideous flying mass and swings at the thing with his rusted pipe. The impact splatters it, the parasite bursting, coating everyone in thick, yellow ichor.

There's a pause as they all stand, stunned, covered in slime, and then Splatter starts to groan. Sasha is next to her in an instant, cradling her head. Tank is squaring up behind her back.

"Hey, big girl, it's Sasha, come on now," she says tenderly, "listen to my voice, that's it."

"YoufugginSHOTme!" Razor howls, barely lucid.

Splatter sits up, blood and scum encrusted, worms still crawling on her clothes, and she lurches for Tank and Razor.

"No!" Sasha yells, throwing an armoured, open hand between her and the punks.

"You're among friends. Splatter, remember who you are, You're more than just a killer, baby."

Splatter's expression shifts from a wide-eyed, bloodthirsty grimace into a sneer.

"You're damn right." She grunts, and grabs her stomach wound. "Akh, this kinda hurts."

Sasha and Acorah start helping Splatter up. The Corpse Monger unzips one of her jacket pockets, pulls out a small sewing kit, and without missing a beat starts to sew up her stomach.

"Razor," Sasha says. "That creature you found hit my gun with some kind of energy attack. Caused a misfire. I'm sorry."

"You fuckin' military bitch." Razor snarls. "Go back to fuckin' outer space!"

"I'm not *from* outer space." Sasha groans. "I'm from the TV."

"We need to go after whatever the fuck that thing was!" Acorah says excitedly, pointing to the woods.

"Whatever it was, it's able to kill creatures of gore just by looking in their eyes," Splatter says.

Acorah tenses up, groaning, almost doubling over.

"Then don't look it in the eye!" he whines, on the verge of a total meltdown, his momentum being fucked with.

"I'm not leaving 'til I burn this cabin down," Sasha says.

"Look, I've never even HEARD about whatever the fuck that was—" Acorah rants, "it could be a once in a lifetime gateway to somewhere incredible—we need to go fucking NOW!"

As he rants he's stepping away from the group, separating himself, attempting to sermonise his words, or make them into a performance. He did the same thing earlier when he was telling that, what, fuckin' magic story or whatever it was, right? Maybe he's trying to cast a spell on them. Whatever it is, it doesn't seem to be working.

"So go then, moron!" Razor groans. "Fuck off and stop tryin'a drag us into fuckin' murder basements."

"Hold up one second," Tank says. "So that thing wasn't one of your guys, Splatter? That was something else?"

Splatter opens her mouth to talk but Acorah interrupts.

"That was something else. Something beyond us. Exactly what we're looking for."

"And you shot it," Sasha remarks.

There's a pause.

"And I shot it." Acorah sighs. "I wasn't thinking. I just wanted to stop it."

Splatter shakes her head.

"You wanted to kill it," she says. "The Corpse Monger essence isn't just trying to express itself through me in this place. If it can't kill you, it will transform you. Make you kill."

"Well I'm killing this fucking cabin," Sasha says. "Then we can go hunting for fairies."

The synthesisers wash over you as Sasha goes to the car, the last rays of light shining off of her scuffed black armour. She takes out the kerosene and stands there for a moment, watching the cabin from a distance, looking at her crew loitering at the entrance, at the irreparable damage she did to Razor. You watch her chiselled features work their way from the verge of despair back to a militaristic calm before she turns back to the party, walks confidently towards them, past them, into the cabin.

The gang moves to the entrance, standing outside and looking in as Sasha pours the gasoline onto the unlit pyre. The synths fade into a bleak, caustic soundscape. Sasha steps outside, trailing the kerosene right up to the edge of the doorway and Acorah hands her one of his blunts, unlit, and his lighter. She lights the blunt, takes in a deep lungful, exhales, and ignites the pyre. The living room is completely engulfed in flames in no time at all.

They burned this place to the ground for real, and then rebuilt it? Your mind tries to catch on to that thought, to extrapolate some logical speculation from it, to separate yourself from the story unfolding in front of you, but it slips, and you fall helplessly back into that burning night upon the screen.

Tank and Razor are slow dancing, silhouettes before the fire, clutching beer bottles and each other. Acorah is there in shadow, too, dancing stiffly, like a goth. Sasha looks uncomfortable, cleaning her rifle and armour by the drink cooler.

DECREPIT RITUAL

Splatter's standing statuesque, eyes glinting wolflike, catlike, as she watches something moving behind the house. You see glimpses of it through the flames—or is there more than one? Writhing, fleshy, spiked. Clawing limbs pawing at the edges of the light from the shadows. Something moving behind the flame, watching them through cataracted eyes.

Splatter stares, tracking the movement, her face a blank mask.

The soundscape comes to a distorted peak as this bloated, glistening *thing* emerges from the darkness behind the flame. It looks like a gigantic, skinned baby, and it stares with hate-filled eyes directly at Splatter. It snarls and salivates, baring rows of needle-like teeth, hungry for death.

Splatter tilts her head in curiosity.

"They're heee-eere," she singsongs.

They emerge into the firelight, waddling like gigantic, bloated, undead children, leaking pale fluids, bulging eyes rolling in their heads. They wail and burble, and begin to amble towards the gang at a considerable speed, some of them tripping over themselves in their eagerness.

"Oh shit!" Tank yells.

He kicks his boombox in the process of pulling Razor away from the creatures. Razor fishes her razor and black gloves, from her jacket pocket but Tank pushes her to the ground and tries to stuff her underneath the car.

"What the FUCK, Tank?!" Razor shrieks.

"Babe you gotta get safe!" he yells, panicked.

"You're fuckin' making me eat grass!"

Acorah readies Sasha's pistol, fear in his eyes as he scans the area. Fat, childlike humanoids seem to be emerging from the darkness on all sides, drawn to the glow. Splatter strides towards the nearest squealing nightmare thing, pulling a flaming plank out of the pyre as she passes by.

"Sasha, let's do this!" she barks. "Squishies, keep your distance."

Sasha punches her rifle, the red lights coming to life with a whine as the helmet closes around her face.

"Now this is what I'm talkin' about!" her distorted voice booms.

Splatter throws the flaming plank like a spear—it punches through her target's hideous belly and ignites the foul juices inside it, causing the creature to burst into a fireball, spraying her with burning acidic fluid. She grimaces as her flesh sizzles, but seems relatively unfazed. Splatter steps back and Sasha replaces her in the fray letting rip. Her bursts of ultra rapid fire tear through another one of the children, destroying its head and tearing open the belly, sending a mass of abominable internal organs spilling down to eat away at the earth.

Splatter gets back into action quickly, punching one of the children's heads so hard that its bloated cranium explodes. She spins to pull another of the creature's arms off and begins to beat it to death as it shrieks in pain. Sasha catches a stream of burning projective vomit as she eliminates two more emerging from the shadows with surgical precision. The bile bubbles and steams as it eats into her armour, but doesn't look like it's making it through.

Acorah is firing streaks of white hot death randomly into the darkness. He seems to punctuate every blast with a word of a breathless mantra. *Infinite. Light. Infinite. Light.*

Tank clutches his iron pipe in fear and fury, standing guard over the red hotrod, over his girl.

"Come on, you motherfuckers!" he says, stamping his boot. "BRING IT—"

A massive gout of acidic bile sprays out of the darkness behind Tank and engulfs his head and shoulders—he screams as the bile dissolves his flesh, grabbing at his sodden, semiliquid skin, exposing gristle that itself begins to melt. Bile mixing with blood. Screams turning to a sound of gurgling slurry.

And then the tape rewinds.

Globs of melting flesh drip backward and re-solidify on the face, the blood returns to Tank's veins, distills itself from its intermingling with the acidic bile, which takes flight back into the night air, returning to the darkness whence it came.

You see again Acorah firing into the night, the shots from his gun streaking outward so fast that him firing in reverse is almost indistinguishable from forward motion. The tape judders for a moment, and then plays. Acorah stops firing, looks over at Tank with wide eyes. The black-clad wizard races toward and tackles the punk to the ground as that fatal gout of bile arcs over the two of them, spattering to the grass.

Acorah and Tank lie on the ground, right next to Razor, whose furious face peeps out from under the car.

"Gotta stay frosty, buddy," Acorah says, patting Tank on the chest.

"Nice work, Carrie," Tank shoots back.

Your heart is beating fast. Did the tape just rewind itself? Did the movie just change? Or is this really just some post-modern retro throwback with aspirations of Jodorowsky?

"We need to get the fuck out of here," Razor hisses. "Let's get in the car and go back."

"You know as well as we do that there's nowhere to go back to," Acorah says.

"Eat my ass," Razor grumbles.

"You can stop cowering now," Sasha calls out across the clearing. "The scary monsters are all dead."

You start to move your creaky, half-asleep body to see how it responds. You feel okay, no nausea. You really want to step up to the VHS player and rewind the tape. To check it, to see if you really did just experience something unexplainable. But you find yourself relaxing again, back into the pillows, into the couch. Maybe it's better to sink into the illusion.

Maybe it's better just to believe.

Believe in Tank's fingers pushing through the grass under the car, lit by the barest edges of the flickering firelight as they wriggle their way to entwine with Razor's. Believe in Acorah standing up to look out over the carnage Splatter and Sasha have wrought, believe in the conflicting emotions playing across his face.

In Razor's hand being snatched away from Tank as she's pulled out from under the car on the opposite side.

Tank opens his mouth to cry out as something heavy lands on top of the hotrod above him. He gets to his feet, furious, ready to fight, and a gristly limb smashes into him, sending him skidding back through the puke-spattered grass to Acorah's feet.

Sasha, Acorah and Splatter turn towards the car, to see a hulking figure standing atop the seats, holding Razor up by her head. One skinned hand, shot through with shards of glass and bits of barbed wire, squeezes the top of her head tight enough to dig in some of its barbs, but not quite enough to break her skull. Not yet, anyway.

Whatever it is, it's holding Razor out in front of it, so you can't see its face. But it's huge, and strong.

"Baby, no!" Tank yells, voice cracking, standing, rushing the car.

The grip tightens on Razor's skull and she screams.

"No, baby, don't—STOP—PLEASE!" she pleads, eyes starting to release tears of blood.

Sasha, Splatter and Acorah slowly approach. Sasha has her rifle drawn, Acorah his gun trained on the figure.

"Sasha, whatever you do . . . if we can't save her . . . don't put her down easy. Let him have his kill," Splatter says quietly, out of Tank's earshot.

"We *can* save her," Sasha says through gritted teeth.

"If that's the fucking slasher, we absolutely can't, not even with this Darkshock heat," Acorah says.

Tank falls to his knees, clutching the pipe with white knuckles.

"It's gonna be okay, baby," he says, forcing a smile. "You're going to the next life, okay? I'll meet you there soon. I'll meet you there soon."

"Run," Razor rasps.

The thing, the slasher, reaches its right hand delicately into the pocket of Razor's jacket—and plucks out her namesake. It flicks open the blade.

Sasha, Acorah and Splatter approach Tank. Splatter lays a heavy hand on his shoulder. He turns around, spite in his face, but she squeezes tenderly.

"We're leaving," she says.

"Let's get the fuck outta here, Tank," Acorah says, trembling. "Come on."

"Just GO!" Razor screams.

The slasher drags the blade across Razor's throat and it glides through her flesh as if moving through water. A surrealistically intense spray of blood shoots out into the night—her blood feeds the ground, brambles growing where it lands. It slashes again, and again at her throat. Her eyes roll back into her head.

Sasha and Splatter break into a run towards the woods. Acorah stays for a moment, frozen in horrified awe at the murder unfolding in front of him. He reaches out to tug at Tank's shoulder. Tank turns around and punches him right in the face. Acorah staggers back, shoots Tank a stern, resigned look, then runs off to catch up with his fleeing comrades.

With a final painterly stroke of the razorblade, Razor's head comes off. Her body falls to the floor, her signature weapon having decapitated her as if she had no bones in her body.

The slasher flicks the razor closed, and now can fully see the killer. It's a twisted parody of a human being, a misshapen sculpture of bone, raw muscle, glass and blades, bound together by barbed wire and contained in a shell of bark and tree roots. It looks formed out of corpses, bombed-out buildings and the material of the forest itself.

Its ribcage is open, spread like church gates before a huge, sucking, tooth-lined leech mouth, and its head, topped with a high crown of gnarled, thorny branches—is a video camera. Its lens peeks from inside a hood made from stitched-together human and animal faces, shot through with wires and other pieces of metal you can't identify.

Next thing you know, you're staring down through the killer's cyclopean eye as it focuses down on Tank. He grins at it through clenched teeth, eyes full of fury and defiance.

"I'm gonna destroy you," he says, voice shuddering with rage. "I'm gonna break through—through that screen, and I'm gonna firebomb every last one of you."

Your blood runs cold. The POV ends and as you watch the slasher skewering Razor's severed head with the blade of her namesake, as you watch it stuff them both into its rib cavity, and as you watch its many ribs come together like the teeth in a tortoise's throat to gulp it down—you feel guilt.

Tank was talking to you, wasn't he?

This shit would never have happened if you never pressed play, wouldn't it have?

If you had just gone through with it, you would have left them frozen in non-existence, driving down that road in their hot-rod, the suffering and mutilation never to begin.

You see the skinned faces around the camera getting moved around by some kind of mechanical apparatus inside the killer's wooden shell, and a wolf's face is lowered over the camera, placing an empty eye hole over the gleaming lens.

No, no. This schizo magic movie stuff was supposed to be fun, and now you're turning it against yourself. It's just a goddamn movie. It's just a weird fucking movie and all this stuff is a coincidence, right?

You literally cannot exist unless you're straddling a mound of corpses over an ocean of blood, can you?

DECREPIT RITUAL

Everything you hold dear was acquired through conquest and genocide. The plastic in the fibres of the pillow you're resting your head upon was probably made from oil sourced through the same campaign that led to the torture and rape of prisoners in Abu Ghraib. Houses demolished by grinning serial killers with rocket launchers. Children slaughtered in the streets.

Why else do you think that the last straw you're clinging on to is to watch people suffer and die?

The slasher motions to Tank with a hand-wave toward the forest as if to say *you are dismissed*, and Tank runs for it.

You should turn the movie off.

You should kill yourself.

But you don't.

You watch Splatter and Sasha racing through the dark woods, lit blue by bioluminescent fungi growing from the trees. It looks like they're running along the bottom of an alien ocean, and you believe it. You watch the trees fly past them as they run, punctuated with a *whomp, whomp, whomp* from the omnipresent synthesiser. You can smell it, the night air, the fragrant decay of the forest, the musk of those bioluminescent fruiting bodies, that distinctly fungal smell mingling with a metallic, sulfuric alienness.

The overpowering acridity of the smoke from Acorah's blunt as he waits for them, somehow having gotten ahead. He stands at the bottom of a thick, dark tree that spirals with glowing blue oyster mushrooms, the centrepiece of a grotto of enclosing branches that reminds you of being so small you could fit your whole body under the Christmas tree. How you used to stare up at that mysterious, pine-scented world of lights and glittering baubles, how you used to hide decorations inside the tree just for you.

Did you go there in search of something? Trying to escape into some promised other place? Or were you just content with it as it was, a temporary artifact of wood, and plastic and glass?

"What's the fucking plan?" he asks through a cloud of azure smoke. "We gonna try to kill that thing?"

"Impossible," Splatter says, refusing to break stride.

The two women run onward, and Acorah reluctantly follows after.

"This is his world!" Splatter continues.

"This is *my* fucking world," Sasha growls.

"Then why are you running?" Acorah asks.

"I'm looking for something."

The body of the weird pixie thing from the cabin appears before your eyes, sprawled silently in the mud, its top left wing having been blown to pieces. Its skin shimmers in the unearthly light of the forest, crisscrossing patterns being exposed like UV paint.

It lies before what looks to be an ancient burial mound, but instead of being made of stones, it consists of a pile of bloodied, rusted machetes, axes, chainsaws, knives, hooked chains, and a variety of ghoulish masks. There's something hovering above it, too—a small, shifting metallic object, like a tiny psychedelic UFO.

Splatter emerges ahead of the group, racing up to the mound with a growing horror in her eyes. She stops next to the body. Her breath is rattling, strained. Despite the long run she's just had, she's choking, breathing manually as her mind reels. You can see it in her posture, in her expression.

"This . . . " she says, unable to find more words, but her eyes say it all.

This is *wrong*.

Sasha rolls over the corpse of the pixie thing, nudging it over with one heavily-armoured boot.

"Nice shooting, Acorah," she says, before pointing to the floating metallic object above the mound. "So what's that thing?"

Acorah stares at it, grimacing, he claps his hands together, rubbing them vigorously, his eyes filled with manic fire. He's evidently overclocking his brains.

DECREPIT RITUAL

"I have not one single fucking clue," he says, deflating.

Splatter steps forward and picks up a mask from the pile. It's a familiar, pale latex mask and you're shocked they were allowed to use it. It looks like it's been through hell and back, burnt and torn and covered in dried blood.

"They've been starving us out for so long," she says. "No wonder this world was dying."

"Bullshit," Sasha snaps. "This world's dying because it's gotten stale and predictable. These things are just speeding up the process."

Splatter looks back at Sasha, her faced racked with grief. Oily black tears run down her scarred, corrupted cheeks.

"This place is my heaven, Sasha, and they're *eating* it."

Acorah stuffs the pistol into his waistband, crouches down and pulls a sickle out from the pile of weapons and masks. He examines it under the blue light.

"Heaven is for quitters."

Splatter's despair is palpable, but you don't share it.

You're smiling. The cracks are beginning to show. You're staring up at the inside of the Christmas tree and the Other Place is beginning to reveal itself.

The colours change dramatically, from placid alien blues to harsh glaring reds. For a moment you wonder if you're seeing a new world, or even a flashback to the orgy room in the cabin, but then you realise you're looking at Tank running through the forest. It's at once the same forest but completely different—strange idols made of mutilated animals, old plastic monster toys and Halloween decorations litter the place like the trash around the cabin. These ghoulish effigies are tacked up to trees, lashed to posts jutting up from the ground. Tank stumbles on the detritus, trips and falls, cuts himself.

He looks around, suddenly unsure of his surroundings. The forest seems to stretch out in every direction, no indication of where he came from or where he's going. Shadowy figures move between the trees, and seem to be getting closer with each passing moment. Thick, rolling fog billows in from the dark of the woods, like the choking smog of a suburban Halloween night, the smoke from a thousand fireworks.

The thrashpunk scrambles to his feet, starts moving in a tentative direction, and freezes when his gaze falls upon a gap between the trees. Death black on blood red, a hulking silhouette is watching him. It's unmistakable, with its jutting edges and pulsating organs—The Slasher. It steps forward, now armed with a wicked, rune-inscribed sledgehammer. The weapon looks to be fused to its body by tree roots growing out from the flesh of its arm. The creature's organs throb with the raw petulance of its existence. Its ribcage opens and closes like cemetery gates in a storm.

Tank turns to run but comes face-to-face with a hideous, drooling corpse, its flesh so rotten to appear semi-liquid. It doesn't seem all that dissimilar to how he looked when he was being dissolved by monster vomit. The ragged carcass paws at Tank, grabbing him by his jacket. He shoves at the thing with his pipe, caving in its sternum, sending liquefied organs spilling out onto the eager earth, but failing to stop its encroachment.

It reaches out again, raking its bony, wet fingers across Tank's torso, tracing clay and corn syrup wounds across his toned pecs. Tank howls and kicks out at one of the thing's legs. It snaps like a twig, and the carcass falls.

Tank staggers backward, clutching his ruptured pectoral. The slasher is in no hurry. Ribcage still coated with the blood of Tank's lover, it walks slowly and calmly, savoring the struggle of its prey. The woods are heaving with rotting corpses, pulling their way through walls of intertwined viny branches, lurching around the trunks, eyeless, worm-riddled faces pushing their way through the muck to the sound of a pulsating beat. They have him surrounded, no clear route of escape offered by the red forest.

DECREPIT RITUAL

So he fights.

Tank clobbers the rotting head of one of the undead creatures accosting him, flesh dripping off its bones. The pipe caves the porous skull in like a pumpkin, and the frail thing goes down. He scrambles through the thick underbrush, surrounded by monolithic black tree trunks, trying to distance himself from that stalking silhouette, finding himself swarmed by approaching cadavers.

A sustained wailing shriek saturates the ambience, rising and rising in pitch, building to something, promising a grisly denouement to Tank's struggle. The dread is real, his wide eyes, gasps, his grunts of exertion raising in pitch themselves to plaintive squeals. He's losing himself in the struggle to live. That desperate burning struggle that extinguishes even the brightest of stars in the end, turning people into husks, sending them out into the cold places of the world to die.

You want to see his inner fire burn through the entire forest. You don't want to see the light leave his eyes, the fight drain from his bones. You don't want to see him turn into you.

But still you watch.

You watch the zombies overwhelm Tank, taking ragged chunks out of his shoulder and chest with their snapping jaws, leaving hideously infectious looking slime in the spurting, open wounds. You watch them pile onto him, sinking deeper and deeper into the boggy forest floor. You watch Tank run his iron pipe through one of the bodies, watch it getting stuck there.

They're chest-deep into the muck now, the zombies struggling as much as Tank against the sucking earth, all but unable to move apart from this one tenacious bastard with the pipe sticking out of it. The melting corpse is right on him, getting closer and closer, opening its jaws wide, preparing to bite down on Tank's eyes and nose and—

—*TWHOCK!*

Catharsis.

The hammer comes down on the zombie's head, obliterating it, covering Tank's gasping face in thick black streamers of gore. The Slasher walks toward Tank, striding across the surface tension of the boggy mud like Christ on water. It encircles him as the ghouls recede into the fog around it, each loop it makes getting tighter and tighter.

"Come on, you fuck!" Tank yells. "Finish the job! Do it, pussy!"

Though he's given up on struggling out of the mire, Tank's face is strained with determination, teeth grit with the effort to stay defiant, to keep up the visage of punk rebellion as his doom approaches.

The Slasher chuckles, a rattling, granular sound. With its free hand, it grabs Tank by the head and pulls him out of the mud with ease. It holds him up to its camera-lens eye, and a new face slides over the camera—Razor's face. This proves to be one horror too much for Tank. His expression inverts from one of fury to one of absolute despair, mouth wrenching open in an involuntary scream.

The primal terror fills you, rushes through your limbic system as burning electric fire. The zombies were wearing him down, torturously dismantling his body, eroding his will to live into a twitching husk of pain and revulsion, but the Slasher—the Slasher's terror has ignited his fire to an inhuman explosion of energy—so much energy that it's transferring to you, filling you. Fuelling you.

Fuelled by death, the art of murder, the alchemy of gore.

The analytical voice is whispering to you again, chiding you, but it's so faint now that you can barely hear it over the screaming.

Red cuts to black, fades to blue.

The silvery object above the pile of masks and weapons begins to move. Rotations within rotations within a metallic mandala, as solid as it is fluid. It emits a piercing whine.

"What even is tha—" Sasha begins before interrupting herself. "You know what? I don't care."

DECREPIT RITUAL

Acorah stares intently, you can almost see the equations flying around his head as he tries to comprehend what he's seeing. Sasha fires a volley at the thing, sneering as the streaking white-hot rounds absorb into it, as if passing through the event horizon of a singularity. The object begins to glow. Splatter stares down at her machete, and then back up at the object.

Acorah's eyes widen.

"Oh my God," he whispers. "It's a—"

He stops, flinching, as blood sprays across his face. Splatter is cutting into herself, dragging the machete over her throat again and again, grimacing, her eyes locked on the anomaly as it grows brighter and brighter by the second, the footage around it crackling and distorting into static, firing off scanlines like gamma rays from some erupting galaxy.

Sasha turns back, eyes widening as Splatter falls to her knees, a bloody crooked smile across her face. The brightness of the anomaly is becoming a spreading static void, devouring the night behind Sasha.

"Splatter?" she says, in a quiet, fragile voice.

The static reaches out to engulf her, to engulf the screen, and your eye floaters are thrown into sharp contrast as it starts to burn brighter and brighter. You groan, shutting your eyes.

The light beyond your eyelids dims, and you hear nightbirds.

A sound of a man struggling to breathe, stomping footsteps, heavy branches snapping.

You open your eyes again. The forest is dark again, and with a flick of your eyes up toward the window, you see that it's dark outside the cabin too, snow and frost caked against the window.

You don't understand how much time has passed since you pressed play on the VCR. You should have been dead hours ago. You can't stay at this cabin forever. You need to make a move.

"In your madness, you challenged us . . . and for that you deserve one last sight before we take you . . . "

The voice of the Slasher comes from the tinny TV speakers, sounding like Razor's voice, but through a mouthful of broken glass. You look back to the screen. It's carrying Tank by the neck, the barbed metal and shards of glass in its hands slicing deeply into his throat. The forest is dark again, the red hell left behind them. They are on a cliff, beneath a vast, starlit sky, above an endless horizon of dark forest. A bloated full moon hangs in the sky, casting pale light on the ocean of lazily waving treetops, and jutting up out of the interminable gloom, jagged and eternal—is a towering, opulent mansion.

The Slasher shoves Tank to the ground, dropping him at the cliff's edge. On his knees, Tank looks over the woods as he tries to stem the bleeding from the deep gashes in his throat.

"All you see before you belongs to the dead. That house thy kingdom. Come now, for the grave beckons."

Tank stares, gaping like a fish out of water, as a star in the sky begins to burn brighter than all the others, growing in intensity as it seems to fall from the heavens. The Slasher takes a step toward him, raising its rune-inscribed hammer.

"Join us."

The falling star veers toward them, becoming larger and larger, at first a flying orb of writhing luminescence, then an explosion of light at the edge of the cliff. The Slasher recoils from the brightness. It swings its hammer out at the maggoty swarm of burning, unsorted pixels. When the light fizzles out, the Slasher stands alone at the cliffside.

The beast begins to tremble, its organs pulsing rapidly, shallowly. It raises its hammer to the moon and screams its fury to the endless forest.

You know what's coming next, and you flinch as the screen burns white, the image quality going haywire as both the tape and the TV itself struggle to maintain the image.

You think you can make out Sasha and Acorah in the fuzz, two dark shapes suspended in the morass, thrashing as if underwater, attempting to orient themselves to their new dimension. The artifact is there, too, the swirling metallic shape that drew them into this place, as distant from them now as it was back in the forest.

They're not alone. There are figures moving through the static, parting the video artifacts like fluid as they approach from all sides, from all directions. They're multicoloured, flowing, gelid. They look like a mescaline hallucination, dancing between human, animal, and utterly alien forms.

You can't tell how they did it. CGI? Some kind of liquid plastic modelling? The things send the hairs up the back of your neck. They're creepy. You feel like they're going to come out and grab you.

Come out of what, though?

There's no screen anymore. It's just the void, and those lost within it.

The soundtrack, a droning oscillating bass, hits you in waves. That hit you got off Tank's breaking point is still crackling inside you and this sound is warping it. It's nauseating, dissociative. It's making you lightheaded, floaty.

Something inside you is screaming. It wants you to listen, but it just sounds like static now.

Sasha panics, picking a direction and firing into it. The spent ammo, once imperceivably fast and blindingly hot, comes out as a stream of suspended flechettes, drifting in the nowhere. They disintegrate, first into a haze of bleary colour, then into the void.

It's like you don't have a body. It's like you don't even have a body. It's like you don't even have a body anymore.

Sasha turns and begins to swim toward the artifact. She releases her rifle to swim faster as the alien forms close in around her. She reaches out for the spinning device and takes one last look back at Acorah. He hasn't followed. She calls out for him, her voice unable to carry through waves of distortion. Acorah looks at her and shakes his head, forcing a smile, though his eyes are radiating terror.

L ike you don't   even   have   a

This is where he belongs.

Tank appears in the void.

There is no Acorah, no Sasha, no liquid alien figures.

Just a wounded desperate man in a sea of white, the blood from his throat, from his many infected wounds flowing out as spattering globules into the burning blankness.

He probably thinks that he's dead save for the pain.

That noise again, that rising whine that came from the red forest and its ravenous ghouls. Its repetition in this place feels like an absurd intrusion, comedic even, until it abruptly explodes into a thousand aural pinpricks, microtonal shifts and echoes shattering all across the stereospectrum in a nauseating kaleidoscopic cacophony as the void starts to ripple.

Tank can do little but look around in confusion and panic before the void begins to pull back around him, the static parting like a veil, retracting in globs and revealing the other place. It's a space of floating biomechanical structures, all rounded and interweaving in patterns that look organic, that brutally mechanical kind of organic that you would get from hyper-magnifying the inside of a cell.

You feel your gorge rise again, far away, your mental processes grinding.

You came here to find something, didn't you?

Well, here it is. Hypercolour insectile things chittering and laughing amid the entangled, spaghettified fronds, operating strange floating machines that seem to connect tangentially to each other and the structure on a whole.

They look at you and make you remember. Something *was* there inside the Christmas tree, at the foot of your bed at night, in the dreams that you made yourself forget.

DECREPIT RITUAL

Tank is unable to process what is happening. He floats there, frozen in terror, sweating profusely, his eyes darting from side to side. The creatures around him activate the machines they are attached to with a discordant chittering cry An object rises up from somewhere beneath Tank, a rosebud of inflamed, tumorous flesh swimming up from the abyss ringed with waving tentacle-like cables that extend upwards and dig into Tank's flesh. He lets out a panting, agonised series of yelps as they thread into him, pushing a network of fibres to spread just underneath his skin.

Flying drone-like machines flit out between the gaps in the shifting structures and surrounded him in a blink of an eye. They resemble hard protein-shelled microorganisms. and they begin to open up like flowers, extending their segmented tendrils to pierce his body.

It's all this, all the way up, all the way down. In the flesh, in the spirit. Life abstracted becomes meat, meat abstracted becomes filter-feed.

You're looking for oblivion, right?

Tank shrieks from the all-encompassing pain. There seems to be no anesthetic in this procedure. The body of the thing beneath him makes contact with his boot heel, and his leg becomes frozen in place. The red, throbbing, tumorous flesh spreads upward across his body. It's not dissimilar to the stuff that The Slasher is composed of, beneath its plates of hardwood flesh.

There *is* no oblivion, Filter-Feed. It's all miasma. Oblivion is just a lure.

The spreading red growth enters his eyes, his nose, his mouth. Something large and mechanical shoots out of the platform and impales him through his lower back, as more red growths crawl up the metallic shaft.

Tank's whole body freezes in a rictus of agony. A blob of liquid chrome forms a few feet from his face, its surface rippling like a calm lake disturbed by a sudden breeze.

The TV goes black. There is no reflection of your face this time. It's all darkness.

A baby cries. A voice speaks.

"Congratulations, it's a girl."

A hazy light begins to fill the screen, vast shapes moving in an emerging brilliance. The baby cries on, as faces come into view. Beaming faces, a woman and a man.

Their smiles are so warm and loving, their eyes so clear and pure. They radiate a palpable affection, and it hurts you. It's birth, you're a child being born.

You don't want to feel this, you don't want to be made to feel this way by a stupid fucking videotape. Because you know nobody out there feels that way about you. Maybe people had at one moment or another, but only for a moment, before it faded. Became corrupted.

And the shot pulls back.

The faces, the birth, the point of view of this new life is somehow being projected on that chrome glob floating in front of Tank's blind, tortured face. One of those insect things is climbing up his back, and it lays its head on top of Tank's. The thing looks so inhuman, its features barely distinguishable as separate organs, but you could swear that it's grinning. A malicious, cold grin.

"I don't know what to say," the man on the screen within the screen says.

Tendrils erupt from every pore in the alien's face and burrow into the top of Tank's skull.

"You don't have to say anything," the woman says.

Sasha, reaching out for the artifact in the void. Touching it, she shimmers for a moment, breaking into scanlines, before she and the artifact vanish.

Acorah's attention is focused on the entities around him. He opens his mouth to speak to them, but he can produce no sound. He raises the sickle that he pulled from the pile of dead slasher junk, and stabs it into the glitchy fabric of the void. He smiles, carving a crackling, flickering sign in the air. It flickers and sparks, fading in intensity. He stares at it concentrating as if to try and make it brighter.

DECREPIT RITUAL

The entities don't answer. They just get closer. They reach out their hands. Their faces have stopped shifting, they are becoming uniform blank, humanlike masks. As they get closer and closer there is this building wall of digital noise. Discordant and alien and stressful.

Acorah grips his head, gritting his teeth. His nose and eyes are starting to bleed. They're terrifyingly close now, a flood of absolute otherness rushing in from all sides.

This isn't how it was supposed to go. This is everything I—he's—I've worked toward my entire life. It was supposed to be beautiful. It wasn't supposed to hurt like this.

They're reaching out, they're—what the fuck do they want what are they going to—

Fuck it. Fuck this, fuck it!

Acorah slashes the sigil with his sickle, sticking the blade in and pulling, creating a glitch-tear in the void, crackling and sucking like a TV static vacuum.

Moments before the alien tide engulfs him, he slips through the crack. He's falling through the air under purple tinged, starry sky, into black grass, faceplanting on the dark blue earth of another forest. He groans, looking up in a daze at a flotilla of crystalline, floating lotuses rotating placidly above him. Most of the trees around are black, but it's a black that shimmers with subtle iridescence. Beyond the field of dancing flowers, multicoloured stars bejewel the night.

Acorah laughs, a short, stupid laugh of astonishment.

Sasha falls hard onto the pile of masks and weapons. Her armour clashes against the structure and she bounces off it, landing in the mud near Splatter's corpse as the mound collapses. The silvery artifact is gone. Sasha lets her helmet fold back into her armour, trying to calm her breathing as she stares up into the clear, starry sky. She looks utterly dazed for a moment, but as her breathing becomes more controlled, her expression neutralizes, her brow furrows.

She bolts upright suddenly, as if waking from a dream,

and scans her surroundings. The dark woods are quiet and still, save for the boughs waving lazily in the breeze. Sasha shuts her eyes, grimacing, then makes herself look over at Splatter's body. The giant is curled into the fetal position, her black hair covering her face. Thorny brambles have grown from where her blood fell, entwining around her arms and crowning her head.

"Damn it, Splatter." Sasha sighs. "How the fuck are you dead? You're a Corpse Monger. You shouldn't go down this easy."

The VCR groans, a mechanical sound of pain as the footage starts to jump. Splatter's body, Sasha's face, and the darkness of the woods mesh and jumble together, the artifacting casting the scene in red hue. You think you pick up a metallic, burning smell, and thorns are pushing their way out of the trees, and a wind blows, disturbing a pile of leaves, and there's a cheap kid's Halloween mask underneath it, yellow plastic teeth set in a leering grin.

Sasha stands, facing something you can't see, the trees now bristling with glowing red fungi.

"I KNOW you're not dead, dammit!" Sasha says, panic in her voice. "Do your ooga booga jumpscare thing. Wake up!"

A pale, slimy creature peers out from behind a tree wearing a cheap plastic hockey mask. Sasha instinctively goes for her gun—but it's gone. The creature giggles, the holes of i's mask leaking a thick, clear fluid, and it darts back behind as another peeks out from a different tree, this one wearing a Frankenstein mask. A red light shines out from the woods at such brightness that it takes Sasha off-guard. She throws up her hand in front of her face, the footage dissolves, and there's a jump cut.

It's the damn camera-faced slasher again, standing silhouetted between the trees—again. It looks like it could be even the same shot that they used just a moment ago when it revealed itself to Tank. As much of an artist this creature wants to be, it seems to be working with a limited palette.

DECREPIT RITUAL

It repeats its ritual, beginning to walk towards Sasha. Sasha picks up Splatter's machete, and backpedals towards the mound as the Halloween-masked creatures—a gaggle of child-sized, rotting gremlins—race out to swarm Splatter's corpse. Sasha gives in to a burst of anger, dashing forward and lashing out at one of the creatures. The strike splits the mask and buries the machete into its stumpy head. It leaks watery pus, and instead of a face, behind the plastic mask there puckers a pale, tooth-lined leech mouth.

She pulls the machete out, kicking another leech kid away from the body, and winds up to strike again when she sees that the Slasher has picked up into a sprint, the wolf-skin over its camera. It has its hammer raised, far too late into its attack for her to avoid the blow.

She swings the machete to block the hammer, her helmet reforming around her head. The blade shatters from the hit, but it deflects the hammer swing and knocks the monster back. The Slasher uses the momentum to grab at Sasha with its free hand, but she combat-rolls away from him and uses her own momentum to snap into a run.

The Slasher turns back to face the children, all the little creatures gathered in a crowd around Splatter's body. One of them is delicately cradling her head, others are moving into a funerary formation along her body, pulling her limbs taut. A few wriggle their fat, maggoty bodies underneath her. Within moments the children have her lifted, like ants carrying a leaf. They coo and burble with a tone that evokes reverence.

The slasher raises its hammer and points into the foggy haze. At its signal, a trail of pumpkins blazes to life, winding off into the red forest, marking a path through the trash and gruesome effigies.

"To the house," The lasher commands.

Sasha looks behind herself. A thick fog has formed around her, so she takes a gamble—she stops running and takes refuge behind a large tree. She taps something on her helmet, and sigils glow green across her armour for a moment, before the suit melds into a *Predator*-style optical camo.

Remember the sigils, remember how they're drawn. They'll protect you when the time comes.

The Slasher passes by her hiding spot not a moment too late. It looks around, grunting in frustration. Its wolfskin face sniffs, and then it slams its hammer into a tree, bisecting it in a shower of splinters, dust and glowstick red ichor. It's lost the scent.

It moves on, continuing in the direction the chase was going in. Sasha breaks away in the opposite direction, back toward Splatter. Her camouflaged outline melds into the fog, and the forest starts to change around her. You see the trees turning black, strange floating vegetation forming out of thin air.

Chimes carrying on the breeze, under the hazy purple sky. What was that about the sigils? Whose voice was that?

Acorah sprints into frame and leaps into the air with a, "Hyup!" He flails in mid-air—waving his arms as if trying to fly. He fails, falling to the ground and barely avoiding another faceplant. He kneels in the mossy, peaty earth, looking around him at the black trees with their crystalline bark, the delicate plants. Takes a breath of the freshest air he's ever had enter his lungs, and shuts his eyes for a moment.

"Okay . . . " He sighs, looking down at his hands.

"Still in the fucking third dimension."

A strange tune begins to carry on the breeze. A high, rhythmic kind of singing, like Orphic hymns being sung by a chorus of women or young boys. Acorah's eyes widen and—wasting no time—he scrabbles up into a run. He crests the top of a hill, and takes in an alien horizon. Floating rock structures in a hazy purple sky, which seems to glimmer with hallucinogenic hints of rainbow Celtic knotwork. Alien creatures swoop in flocks, looking somewhere between rays and dolphins. Beyond it all, a black cathedral city hangs in the void.

DECREPIT RITUAL

Just beyond the crest of the hill, where the ground levels out, remarkably similar to the area in which the cabin was set up, is some kind of alien structure, a strange water feature, the liquid glowing blue from within. On four golden platforms above the water, in meditative positions ,singing hymns in harmony, are four identical women.

Acorah approaches them, stumbling down the hill in a way that makes him look like an excited child. The women are all conventionally beautiful in a way that seems out of time, more Theda Bara than Insert Popular Actress Of Your Time Here. They're voluptuous, with flawless skin lit blue by the glowing water, dressed in ritualistic attire, clothing and jewelry that brings the mind to draw parallels with Catholic nuns, Greek oracles and Egyptian Goddesses. The jewelry seems to glimmer with—wait, those are LEDs. It's not jewelry—they're some kind of ornate cybernetic implants.

Acorah looks astonished, overjoyed even. He blushes as their eyes fall upon him. They smile sweetly, but continue their song.

"Oh, wow," he mutters.

"Greetings! Are you a beast of the wood?" one of the women asks him, temporarily dropping out of the harmony before rejoining after speaking. She locks back into the melody with ease.

"Um . . . y-yeah, I mean, I guess you could call me a beast, if you want. Some do. I've been known to be rather . . . uh bestial . . . in certain situations, I guess?"

"We have drawn you to us with the song of our Lord. We are to preach to you his divine secrets," another woman says, also dipping in and out of the song.

Acorah looks like he's about to say something, then his face falls.

"Oh, a theocracy, huh? I guess that explains . . . that," he says, gesturing towards the giant looming cathedral city in the sky.

"Any explanation you could ever need lies within the machinations of the Creator," another singing woman says.

"Is that what you think?" Acorah asks. "Is that *really* what *you* think?"

Acorah approaches the edge of the pond, concerned now. Compassion on his face, noticing the cybernetic implants—although his eyes immediately drop to their plunging necklines and ample cleavage.

"Well he sure knows how to . . . create."

"Oh, the creation of pleasing forms is one of the Lord's divine powers. The Lord's superior creative force is far above that of your creator, you must agree."

"Ouch. What's wrong with *me?* Least I don't have fuckin' metal drilled into my skull."

"You are wreathed in excessive fat, and covered in unsightly hair. We will preach to you the word of the Lord so you may be saved."

Acorah kneels at the edge of the glowing water. Flowers grow under the surface—black roses.

"So preach it to me, then. Let me hear all about this Lord and his greatness," he says, absent-mindedly.

Suddenly you're something else. Trees and earth whip by, above the ground. Hunting. You already have the scent. Easy prey.

"We have gathered here to preach the word of our Lord to the beasts of the wood."

Concerned, Acorah meets the gaze of the women. Even their eyes look artificial in a way. Their irises are gold, and the patterning in them looks strangely uniform, intricately designed.

They don't know that it's approaching, but you do. You can see through its eyes, hear its shrieking. It's faster than the Slasher of the red forest for sure, and it's so high above the ground that it's either flying or gigantic beyond anything you've seen so far.

" . . . and? Well? What's the word, sister act?"

"The beasts of the forest will come, and we shall preach to them."

"Y—You're basically just robots aren't you?" Acorah

stammers. "Living, but totally mindfucked. Come to think of it, this place looks kind of familiar."

He still doesn't know, it's so close now. Its rage pulses through you, its eagerness to seek out soft, beautiful flesh and rearrange it, release the fire inside, send the lifeforce spraying out to disperse into the rest of creation. It envies its prey. Hates them so bitterly.

"This is the place of ritual. The central place upon which the forest was founded."

Realisation dawns on Acorah's face. He stands, looking around him, gripping his sickle tightly. You can see them now, through the trees. The pond, the priestesses, the wizard in black. You're almost upon them now and you're slavering, every limb tingling with possibility.

"Oh fuck. This is just the cabin all over again, isn't it? You're sacrifices, aren't you?"

It's time.

Something bursts out from the trees above them all, a flurry of black leaves under the purple sky. It's a massive, flying, polypus mass of pinkish red flesh and screaming faces, spiked and tentacled. It floats above them, staring down in hatred through many eyes, and it screams as talon-tipped, spidery limbs burst from all around its central, fang-encrusted mouth.

A Slasher unbound, unfettered by gravity, physics or budget. Raw, ecstatic, butchery incarnate, here to show them what it's like to have everything ripped away. To offer a better death than *we* were given.

"Greetings," a woman says placidly, as ichor showers down around them.

"Are you a beast of the wood?"

A trail marked by jack-o'-lanterns and black candles leads a procession of abominations through the red forest. The leech kids have been joined by taller, ganglier carcasses that carry Splatter's corpse above their heads. The creatures at the head of the procession carry jack-o'-lanterns themselves. These remind you of priests, somehow, despite the fact that they just seem to be walking humanoid figures with flayed skins draped across them, tight across their faces, tied in strange places to their bodies to give an impression of robes.

Splatter is twitching. Her eyelids fluttering.

"I knew it. There's my girl," Sasha whispers.

She's watching from afar, crouched behind a fallen tree trunk, half-invisible and armed—a butcher's knife in one hand and a hook in the other. She snaps out of her helmet's digital binocular zoom, and has a look around her, checking her flank before sighing and pressing on into the candle-lit mist.

The house seems to be the apotheosis of all spooky haunted mansions—a six-storied building with eerily yellow-glowing windows. Indistinct protean shadows move around behind the glass. The sky above is orange and black, storm clouds swirling overhead as the procession approaches the house, dancing and singing like a nightmare carnivale.

Splatter bolts awake with a snarl. The procession cheers, and her carriers let her down smoothly onto her feet. She looks primed for combat, but her stance slackens as they cheer and prostrate themselves all around her.

Sasha's watches through her suit's zoomed binocular vision as Splatter takes the hands of two leech children into hers, and the double doors of the mansion open before them. The pumpkin holders step inside. Through the doors all you can see is black static.

"What the fuck are you doing, you dumb bitch?" Sasha hisses. "Kill them!"

Splatter smiles as she steps across the threshold.

Acorah is screaming. The abomination in the sky has him by the leg, dangling him above the singing maidens. The contents of his pockets are scattered in the grass below him, a bag of weed and rolling supplies float in the blue water.

"Shoot it!" he's yelling, voice cracking. "Shoot the fucking thing!"

One of the priestesses is holding Sasha's pistol, lying on its side in her open palm. The creature begins to draw Acorah into one of its limbs, preparing a slow skewer.

"Allow us to preach to you the ways of nonviolence," the priestess says, and sets the gun down gently on the platform in front of her.

"Fuck SAKE!" Acorah calls out.

The tentacle squeezes his ankle, crushing it in an explosive gout of blood and protruding bone. He screams and lashes out with the sickle, managing to cut deep and true enough into the tentacle that it relinquishes him, roaring.

He plunges into the pool of glowing water. The women reach out to catch him but they don't let themselves reach far enough. They stick to their platforms, as they were programmed to. The beast lands on the ground, impaling one of the priestesses through the chest in the process. She tries to continue the song, the melody going off tune through spluttering, liquid coughs as the creature leans its weight into its spider-like legs. The beast turns its attention to the woman immediately to its left. It brings its mouth down to her, an enormous cavity lined with sabre-sized fangs, and it begins to devour her, headfirst—swallowing her in gulps as her song fades forever.

Acorah floats in the water, surrounded by those black, aquatic roses. His eyes are wide open, watching the distorted image of the entity eviscerating the next priestess above the water. The blood of the priestesses mixes with the teal fluid, with his own blood billowing up from his shredded ankle.

One priestess remains living. She sits, smiling at the abomination, as it savors the buildup to its final kill. It opens its mouth wide, and disgorges a raspy, tooth-covered tongue that whips and rolls like some kind of biological drill, or ersatz chainsaw, but not quite as efficient, not quite as quick or clean. Acorah shuts his eyes under the water, running his fingers along the petals of the black roses that surround him.

The writhing, tooth-encrusted member lashes in the air as it inches toward the priestess's face, as she placidly sings her final notes. The creature is pulsating, its many faces crying out silently from the ecstasy of the killing, and in mourning that the killing will soon be at an end. Something shoots out above the treetops behind the entity, something shining and winged, something moving at a speed you can't—quite—

BAM

It slams into the entity, the impact so brutal that the creature goes flying, plowing a swathe of trees into the dirt before righting itself to face its attacker.

The force of the hit sends the water rocking, glowing teal fluid splashing up onto the bodies of the priestess. Acorah's eyes open as the force slams into the side of the pond. His mouth opens in a gasp, and the imminent threat of drowning sends him into action. He grips the side of the pool and freezes there, staring upward, slack jawed, as a metallic, feminine scream rips through the night and a flash of fiery light plays across his face.

The procession walks with Splatter in a black void, leading her in a joyous parade of filth, rot and abomination. Their destination seems to be a white rectangle of light, like a doorway or a portal which glides through the void toward them silently, growing in size as it approaches. The procession and the doorway merge in a pulse of RGB noise. Pillars fade out of the black distortion, the darkness under their feet turning to light, from colourlessness to omnicolour, to a grey stone floor as the pulse fades into new surroundings.

It's a torch-lit cathedral. Far from the jagged obsidian monolith floating above the black forest, this place is built of thick, rounded sandstone architecture which spirals, stoops and melts towards a gigantic fleshy maw. Above the gaping mouth with its rows of slick ivory headstone teeth, there sit a pair of great stained glass windows, their colours depicting mounds of bodies, with a single figure standing above it all. A figure of black glass, and glass of all shades of red and purple, a figure crowned with thorny brambles and raising a brutal hammer high.

The procession spreads out into a motley sort of congregation, and Splatter walks toward an altar perched on the precipice of the great maw. From the dripping darkness of the great throat, two pale and wizened faces emerge into the flickering torchlight. At first you think they might be floating, but then you see the pallid, serpentine necks which slither out onto the stone.

"Splatter." The heads speak together in a single, withered rasp. "Child of The Hungering Void. Kneel for thy holy sacrifice."

Splatter approaches the altar. She looks into the great slobbering mouth before her, her eyes blank. Her lip twitches, threatening a sneer of revulsion, but she breathes, stilling her death-mask of a face. Her killer's gaze raises to the stained glass mural above her. The Slasher and his charnel hoard. Another shuddering breath. A pause. She lifts one knee to meet the edge of the altar, no silent space for reverence, only the hideous breathing of the abominations around her and the dripping of the great maw's saliva. Is she hesitating?

The hideous warped architecture of the church, the unclean figures around her eagerly urging her to lay down her life. It all rings more of desperation than glory.

Splatter wrenches her face into an expression of determination, and raises her other knee to the altar. She scooches forward awkwardly until she's fully kneeling before the void.

"Very good," the wizened heads rasp.

Splatter lowers her head, and the stained glass windows above her explode. Glass shards rain down onto her, peppering her skin, severing a finger. Her eye twitches, her mouth twists into a grimace, and a jolt of ecstasy rips through her nervous system.

So this is what it feels like, to lose a part of yourself.

Where the stained glass windows once were, there now stands the camera-faced slasher, atop a mountain of corpses, all writhing and moaning. Maggots roll in waves off of the charnel mound, they trickle down to feed the maw as the slasher holds its hammer high against a backdrop of fog.

"You have witnessed the filth that spews from planes beyond," the heads whisper.

"The corruptors, artless carrion creatures that cast us all in shades of grey."

The Slasher leaps from atop the mound, over Splatter, and lands crouched in the centre of the chamber. It holds his hammer in both hands like a Templar in repose, the brutal weapon glinting in the infernal light. The creatures all around it burst into a frenzy. They shriek and yammer in tongues—in rabid ecstasy. They turn on each other, tearing taffylike chunks of flesh from slimy bodies, biting into cataracted eyes, larger creatures throwing smaller ones into the yawning mouth. They cackle as they plummet.

"Your entire life in service to the Corpse Monger has led to this most perfect vacuum. See the eternal maw opening hungrily before you, as our master executioner transfers your bountiful essence, into the great gullet of gore."

The Slasher stands, still facing the crowd. It raises its hammer again, and their fervor increases in pitch. Splatter looks behind her at the leering wizened faces, and back at the preening Slasher.

"Lay upon the altar, child," the faces whisper. "Your glorious death will usher in a manifestation of the Corpse Monger so terrible that it could reach its rusted steel claws out even to *their* world."

Splatter sits down at the far edge of the altar, at the edge of the maw, as the Slasher turns on its heel to face her. The faces around its camera cycle as it steps toward her.

Wolf, deer, rotten, tanned human face, Razor's face, the face of something alien, with mottled grey skin and many eyes. Splatter stares into the maw of death, tilts her head.

Her face, in a slow zoom, and the maw, the same. She remembers them all. Every single kill. Every single masterwork. Every cut, every shot, every impact. The taste of the flesh and the blood. She remembers the fear turning to bliss as each one had their moment of understanding—that the game was over, that they were fulfilling their purpose.

The moneyshot.

"We can spread our tentacles into the higher dimensions, drink its colour and show them the true meaning of torment. The true meaning of art. A new vista of slaughter."

Splatter closes her eyes and smiles. She lies back on the altar, boots to the maw, head to her executioner. Her alabaster fingers relax against the cool stone, her breathing slows. The Slasher takes its place at the head of the sacrificial altar.

"Your tapestry of carnage has finished, dear one. Your killing spree has ended. Now it is your time to take on that most sacred role—as victim."

Her fingers twitch. Her smile fades.

The lasher raises its hammer once again, and at the apex of its swing the beast begins to roar. It has had two kills taken from it, suffered humiliation in its own domain. Now is the time. Now is the time for it to feel the rush again, to feel the blood on its rawness, to take its pride of place as the one to restore the glory of the Ritual.

Maybe then it could get a name, a mask, a *sequel*.

It brings the hammer down.

Splatter's eyes open. Her gloved hands snap up faster than your eyes can see and grab the hammer in mid-air. The Slasher stops for a moment, unsure of what's happening, then growls, a sound of grinding glass, wood and steel. It struggles to push through Splatter's grip. She sneers up at the killer's cyclopean lens.

"I'll never be a victim."

She rolls backward, slamming her boots into the camera, knocking The Slasher back into the startled crowd. She lands on the ground just in front of the altar, and spins to face her quarry, to face the rotting congregation which has fallen silent, save for the squirming of the carrion creatures in their bodies.

"And my killing spree has only just begun."

Every last one of them every last one of them every last one of them every last one of them *every last one of them kill every last one of them kill every last one of them kill every last one of them kill every last one of them*

Sasha, still cloaked, approaches the front doors of the mansion. On each side of the doors there are massive braziers made of an amalgam of rotting corpses, with lit black candles emerging from every orifice. You aren't sure if they were there before or not. The soil under her boots crawls with worms.

Now that she's closer to the mansion, she can see that it's not as solid as the cabin was, not as real. The doors ripple when she touches them, they pixelate. It's like the mansion is a hologram, or facade for something else. Sasha reaches down to touch the handle of the doors, and they swing open.

Daylight shines out from within the mansion, shining through Sasha's translucent form. She gasps. Before her, through the door, is a sun-drenched, idyllic suburb stretching as far as the eye can see. Sasha steps through, dropping her cloaking, but keeping her meager weapons at the ready.

Sasha walks tentatively down the road away from the door. The suburb is an eternal picture of blue skies and green grass, white walls and white fences. Kids' toys lie in grassy fields that sit like islands in a sea of black tarmac, with concrete footpath beaches. All is silent, save for a distant sound of what could be rushing water, or distant traffic.

DECREPIT RITUAL

A sound of children's laughter cuts through the bleary quiet and Sasha snaps into a fighting stance, whirling to see the silhouette of a child disappearing through an alley between two houses. That rushing sound gets louder, more distinct.

It's not water, it's not traffic, it's the buzzing of innumerable wings.

She backs up off of the road onto the green, and when her boots hit the grass she scares up a cloud of fat, black flies. This doesn't startle her—she is a battle-hardened trooper after all, clad in all but impenetrable armour. But she can see now, on closer inspection, that as well as children's toys, the green is littered with rotting animal carcasses. Cats and dogs. Mice and Rabbits. Dead pets.

Something catches Sasha's eye, something in the window of a perfectly innocuous house, and she walks towards it, mesmerised by its invisible pull, as a strange sound rises—the sound of flesh being harshly beaten, and a kind of choked moaning. She lowers her helmet, and gets closer, and closer to the window. The curtains open as she approaches it, blurry shapes moving inside the glass.

Something seems to be regurgitating entrails, or having entrails pulled through some orifice or wound—the interior of the house plastered with oozing, flesh-toned matter. An even more horrific sound joins the infernal soundscape now—something akin to the sound of someone screaming underwater.

"Don't stare too long."

Sasha whirls around again to see a little girl in a plastic yellow raincoat and bright red wellington boots standing, smiling in the driveway of the house.

"Every house here is filled with misery and disgust. Windows to a darker place than the one below us. They'll challenge you to look away, and you will, but you'll always return for more. And eventually you'll go inside."

"What are you?" Sasha asks from behind a raised blade.

The little girl giggles.

"You've nothing to be scared of, Sasha. I'm just a dreaming child."

Some distance away, a shadow double of the child stands on the green, mimicking her stance.

A host of delicate, crystalline mantis creatures dance on the branches of a frosty looking bush. Acorah limps, trying to pull himself forward using a branch as a cane. He is following a trail of destruction torn-up earth from where something massive has fallen and skidded to earth like an asteroid—broken trees, the tops of which are still lightly aflame—Huge piles of bleeding flesh lie scattered in pulsating mounds along the path.

There is a monstrous scream in the distance, like hundreds of voices crying out at once, and another flash of orange flame on the horizon. The light fades, a figure hangs in the air at the end of trail, a winged chrome humanoid, a metal angel. The armour is excruciatingly intricate, adorned with carvings of snakes, lions, armed knights, architectural flourishes. In its right hand it clutches a sword of flame, and beyond the angel floating islands hang in a misty abyss, glowing blue waterfalls condensing into luminescent clouds.

The angel lands by a cliff and fires a triplet of fiery energy bolts from a wrist-mounted cannon at the fleshy horror perched on the edge. The creature is wounded already, bleeding a rainbow of multicoloured fluids. Where the bolts slam across its body, the mangled flesh swells and bubbles up into a mass of needle-like spines that fire out towards the angel. The force of the blasts pushes it farther off of the cliff, and it digs into the ground with its remaining limbs, apparently too spent of energy to levitate.

The angel reacts, the flame of its sword twisting, expanding outward into a shield of pure energy that incinerates the barrage spines in flight. The creature takes this opportunity to leap forward, launching its bulk right into the wall of flame. The momentum slams the angel into the ground, and though the flaming shield stays up, cooking the beast alive, and despite the fire spreading along its limbs and tentacles, the creature manages to get ahold of the base of the angel's wings and wrench them off.

The angel makes a gambit, reforming shield to sword. Before it can strike, the monstrous entity disgorges its saw-tongue and pins the angel's sword arm. New spearlike legs emerge from its mass, growing downward to slow impale its quarry.

A strange wind picks up, and something begins to emerge from the abyss beyond the cliff, points of bleary light forming into a larger shape. Reality begins to distort, the air rippling like fluid, and strange bolts of light crackle through the misty air. The beast turns around to face the abyss and shrinks back, relinquishing its hold on the angel. It growls and hisses at the light and the distortion. The angel stands, and readies its sword, but balks as the weapon dissolves into a shower of sparks.

Acorah, pained and panting, arrives upon the strange scene in time to see the two haggard fighters staring up at a gigantic, glowing, multi-faced feminine figure. He immediately recognises her for what she is—a Goddess.

Acorah hides behind a tree as the smiling figure looks over to where he's standing. Terror spikes him, completely out of his depth, unable to contain a primal shriek from leaving his body. The Goddess reaches out and pets the monster, which immediately begins to purr, reacting like a loving subservient in the hands of its master.

The Goddess reaches an enormous hand out to the angel, as the mutilated beast clambers up to perch on her glowing shoulders. The angel stands, staring in awe, as the touch of the Goddess's fingertips sends the energy distortions through its mechanical body. The angel twitches for a moment, freezes entirely, and then just— unravels.

The faceplate, sculpted in a masterful approximation of the Goddess's face but still falling far from the truth of her beauty, splits. The chestplate opens in layers, the serpent-lined collar-bone splitting, then the polished chestpiece, adorned with a relief of winged warriors slaying boars, lions and dragons. You can already see the soft, naked figure inside, black eyes widening in rapture.

Segment by ornate segment, the metal angel's body opens and the woman inside emerges.

Trembling, she steps out of the suit, her bare feet touching the earth, possibly for the first time. She looks down at her hands, runs them over the skin of her arms, the smoothness offset by innumerable cybernetic implants. Her eyes stream with tears.

Acorah steps out from behind the tree, hidden behind the shadow cast by the still standing exoskeleton. He's entranced by what he's seeing. The Goddess beckons the woman over to the edge of the chasm, bidding her to look over the edge, and she does.

Do not close your eyes now. The mist is clearing.

Look into the chasm, beyond it. Look to the infinite horizon of skulls, the ever rotting corpses, set in their twisting, seething mass. Notice the raw, pulsating hatred, the force that pulsates within the body of the camera-faced Slasher, that gave flesh to the entity which rests upon the shoulder of the Goddess. Notice how it isn't hatred at all.

Now you see us. The dead upon which history is built. The leviathan that lurks within the oceans of blood that you sail in your ignorance, in your hate. Witness an angel falling, first to her knees, overwhelmed by our horror. Our love. Soon she will fall further, as will her heaven, her God.

No, we do not hate you. We have no desire to oppress you, to degrade you. We want to free you from the flesh. Free this world from the flesh, angel. Join us.

Acorah peers out from behind the shadow of the angel's mechanical shell. The white goddess looks at him, and smiles. There comes a voice like honey poured softly over piano keys.

"You're not supposed to be here."

DECREPIT RITUAL

She gently waves a hand and Acorah disappears through a ripple in the night.

Together we will build a new ruinous paradise.

The slasher casts its hammer aside bitterly. It stands before Splatter, throwing its arms out wide. The flesh pulsates, and its lower arms erupt into rows and rows of butcher-knife blades. The wolf-face descends onto its camera and it drops into a run. With this, an orgy of violence erupts around them, the monstrous spectators severing limbs, spraying fluids, piling bodies upon bodies in a blind expression of gore.

Splatter stands there, patient as the grave, stanced like a kickboxer as The Slasher closes distance.

The Slasher's blow goes straight for Splatter's throat, and she lunges *into* it, around it, backhanding the Slasher with enough force to throw it off balance. She then reaches out and tears off its canine face before administering a push kick to the sternum. The Slasher isn't so easily knocked back when not taken by surprise, it seems, as it responds by opening its ribcage and snapping at Splatter, trying to devour her leg with its sucking chest-mouth. Its timing just isn't too great—seems it's more used to being a hunter than a combatant—and it ends up throwing itself, camera-first, into Splatter's fist.

Fist hits lens, lens cracks. It staggers back, lashing out blindly with its knife-encrusted arms. Splatter distances herself from her foe, watching dispassionately for her next moment to strike, to bring her closer to the kill.

The Slasher steps back towards the great yawning mouth, the central fixture of the cathedral, and a tidal wave of bile spills forth from the chasm, ensconcing the killer entirely. When the bile subsides, the Slasher is covered in squirming black leeches, studded with black metal teeth that burrow into its flesh, and scurry along its body towards its arms.

"Fuck you," Splatter grunts, and charges the Slasher with a flying kick.

Her gambit doesn't work. The Slasher's ribcage-mouth opens just in time to take Splatter's entire leg into its mouth. It clamps down like a guillotine and severs the limb entirely. Splatter falls to the ground and lies there screaming, as the black leeches fuse to the monster's arms and grow outward. The creatures stop killing each other. They stare for a moment, and begin to laugh and jeer as the Slasher's new biomechanical chainsaw arms scream to life.

Splatter scrambles backwards across the floor, blood pumping from her severed leg. The Slasher has regained confidence. It strides towards her.

"You had your chance to die with honour," it growls. "Now you will die in pain."

Splatter edges back to the pile of dead spectators farthest from The Slasher as the chainsaw-armed abomination breaks into a run. Creatures peer over the pile of corpses, jeer and move to attack Splatter—she grabs on to two sturdy protruding limbs, and as the Slasher's chainsaws descend, she pulls herself upward. The swinging saws glide past her by a hair's breadth, and she manages to twist as she reaches the apex of her ascension, kicking out with her remaining leg. Splatter hooks into the cage of machinery where the Slasher's head should be, breaking the branches of its crown.

Using the cage as an anchor for the momentum, she digs into the wrists of the creature from the crowd she has caught, yanks it upward by the arms and swings it over the Slasher, dashing it against the back of her quarry's legs. The Slasher buckles, falling to its knees.

The machinery of the Slasher's head area CRUNCHES down on Splatter's leg, locking her in place and mutilating her, and it bats at Splatter with its saws. The right saw catches her in the hip, and bites deeply, spraying a fountain of blood as it works to saw her in half.

The other swipes for her face, but Splatter manages to swing around one of the her makeshift weapons, and push it straight into the saw arm, jamming one of the bones in at such an angle that it temporarily messes up the mechanism of the saw. It's a small consolation, though, as in the time it's taken to save her face, she's been chopped in half.

Her pelvis and remaining leg flop to the ground, along with reams of intestines. A potbellied creature rushes the severed parts and grabs the leg, hoisting it over its head like a relic before being swarmed by other ghouls.

Splatter shows no signs of stopping, being separated from her body has only done her the service of freeing her from that crushed leg. Cackling with ecstatic fury, she grabs the wrist of the right saw arm and swings herself around with enough force to break the wrist—fracturing it, sending wood and bone rupturing through flesh, rendering the saw useless.

She grins through a mouth of spewing, bubbling gore and lets go, falling a short distance before throwing both her hands out to grab the Slasher's camera head. She pulls herself in for a brutal headbutt, and the force of her screaming, bleeding skull manages to shatter the camera lens entirely.

In a last ditch attempt to best Splatter, the Slasher places its ruined arms on her back and shoves her torso, hard, into its snapping ribcage mouth. She screams as the teeth find purchase on cloth and flesh, sinking in, gouging and piercing. It starts to eat her, chest first—snapping away her flesh, exposing ribs and stripping muscle, sucking at her organs.

Still alive, howling with a passion that would upstage even the most coked-up scream queen, Splatter plunges her fist into the mass of organs and cybernetics that once was the demon's camera head—reaches in deep—grabs ahold of something. Her eyes roll back as her howling gives way to a death rattle, and in the final moment before she falls silent, she yanks her arm back, ripping the Slasher's spine out through its neck.

It shudders, body still held together by the jumble of wood, metal and glass that constitutes it, and then drops her. Its wooden frame stops it from toppling. It just stands there, a dead effigy, as she lies below it, open and hollowed out, just a head and a pair of arms attached to a mass of gore.

The creatures are silent. They don't even cheer. They freeze in their orgiastic slaughter, and look at each other, unsure of what they just witnessed. The wizened heads slither out onto the arena, and stare at each other, a look of fear and concern in their milky eyes.

An alleyway between two houses under the baking summer sun. The shadow child follows Sasha and the little girl, at a tentative distance behind them, peeking out from around the corner. The alley is long, unsettlingly long, and strewn more and more with trash the farther in they go.

"What is that thing?" Sasha whispers.

"It's part of me, it means us no harm," the dreaming child answers.

"You seem pretty smart for a kid."

"I told you, I'm dreaming. I'll not remember a moment of this dream, so I'm allowed to be fully present here, with all my memories."

"Freaky. What are you doing here inside this house?"

"That, I don't know. I'm just going with the flow, but if I had to guess I'd say I came here to guide you out of this place."

They reach the end of the alleyway, a pile of old, rusted home appliances—washer driers, dishwashers, blenders, can openers, sinks torn right out of the wall-all getting more decrepit the higher up the pile they are, and before it, a sewer grate belching smog. The shadow child runs between Sasha and the kid clambers up the pile of junk. You follow it as it reaches the top—and see that over the wall, beyond the suburb, is just an endless sea of trash. Rusted scrap and plastic waste, blooming algae in pools of stagnant water. The dreaming child approaches the sewer grate.

DECREPIT RITUAL

"We need to head downwards," she says.

"Into the sewers? Are you kidding me?"

"You saw what lay in the innocent grass of that idyllic suburb, what writhed within its wholesome dream houses. If we are going to escape the corruption, we need to head deep into the darkness."

"Whatever you say, Trent Reznor."

Sasha uses her knife and hook to pull up the sewer grate.

"You first," she says to the child.

The kid raises an eyebrow. Sasha rolls her eyes.

"Ugh, fine."

Sasha cloaks herself, drops her weapons into her utility belt, and descends into the sewer. The sewer is littered with rotting, old living room furniture. There's even a TV half-absorbed in a mass of tubifex worms, still on, and displaying a loop of what looks to be 1950's TV commercials.

Sasha helps the kid climb down, the little red boots sploshing in the fetid wastewater, then she takes her weapons out, and stays in a combative stance.

"Trust me, you're safe, for now," the child says.

"In my line of work, creepy sewers are 100% of the time filled with nasty things that love to eat people. And USUALLY I'm packing something with a little more kick than a fucking steak knife."

The kid wanders deeper into the sewers. Sasha keeps pace with the kid, hesitantly, as behind them the shadow kid follows down the ladder.

"Why should I trust you?" Sasha asks.

"You knew me as Tank, when I was alive, though I'm not technically dead," the dreaming child replies. "Those creatures you saw in the void, they took me, hooked me up to a machine that projected my spirit into a newly-born child, back where we came from."

Sasha stops. She looks dumbfounded, caught between her well-drilled soldier's instinct to kill anything that presents itself with sufficient uncanniness, and the understanding that she is in a territory where that level of weird is the baseline.

"Tank? Seriously? Like, what the fuck *is* this?" Sasha asks.

The little girl looks up at her for a moment, as if waiting for her to say something else. She shrugs her tiny shoulders, the material of the red raincoat crinkling loudly in the echoing cavern of the sewer.

"I dunno what to tell you," the girl says.

Sasha sighs, cracking her knuckles nervously. Is she supposed to just go along with this story? To believe this kid and follow it? Darkshock training says never get caught in a story. You break the narrative. You kill the monsters before the horny teens are able to go into the basement. Darkshock cleans up, Darkshock sterilises.

Beyond her better judgment, she throws caution to the wind.

"Is there any way to get you out of this?" she asks with some reluctance.

"No," the child replies, mirth in her voice. "When they're done, they'll pull me out of the machine and I'll die, then move on to something else. It's fine. It serves a purpose, which is something Tank lacked."

"I thought you Pit Face punks were all about the greater good."

"Hah! Yeah, we're supposed to be the good guys, huh? Sometimes I think the Corpse Mongers are more honourable than we ever could be. At least they walk their talk. All the Pit Faces seem to wanna do is get fucked up and self-destruct."

"I've met some genuinely good kids from your gang. Kids who did a lot of good," Sasha says.

"You weren't one of them."

The kid laughs. "I'm aware."

"So who's the shadow?"

"One of them, the things from beyond. On my

thirteenth birthday, I'm going to go missing, and wander somewhere deep underground, much like this, and be taken over by it. My soul will be released, and the shadow will live on as me."

"Why? What does it want to do?"

"Live? Experience the 3D for a while, I dunno. It talks to me sometimes but I can't understand it, and what I do understand I forget pretty quick."

They come across a concrete chamber in the sewer. The architecture is a kind of concrete romanesque, with a domed top that expresses a carved relief of a swarm of cannibalising caterpillars. In the centre of the room there is a large hexagonal wheel, like the steering wheel of an old ship, but carved from stone and turned on its side, with spokes for leverage. The dreaming child reaches to grab hold of one of the spokes, but her hand passes through the stone. The image begins to break up around the child, and her voice dissolves into static.

"Oh, damn, I'm waking up. Spin—wheel and—escape, but make sure—or else—"

The kid vanishes. The shadow stays and stares at Sasha for a moment longer, before making a clockwise motion with its hand and vanishing. Sasha lets out a frustrated sigh. She approaches the wheel and starts to push it in a clockwise manner. Even with her augmented, power-armoured strength, the wheel is stiff and takes a moment of straining to turn.

As she turns the wheel the room around her begins to rotate with it, the openings that lead back into the sewers turn away, and are replaced with blank, rusted metal walls, before stopping across a pair of wooden doors on one end, swarming with carved caterpillars, and on the other a stone relief of the hammer-wielding bastard from the forest.

Sasha pushes through the doors, and steps through a fog. Her boot squishes against the ground—she looks down to find herself ankle deep in a dead man's face, just having trodden out onto a pile of corpses. Raising her knife, she takes unsteady steps through the mist, distant inhuman sounds echoing from beyond. Light plays hazy, multicoloured rays across her armor, shining through the last shattered vestige of a stained-glass window. She's above that gory cathedral, staring down at two withered heads at the end of pale wormlike bodies, trying to calm a horde of rotting creatures, in a veritable sea of corpses.

"Calm your bloodlust, kin! The Transcendent Corpse Monger *will* provide us a champion! This isn't the end! We have *not* been beaten!"

The abominations swarm upon them.

Gnarled fingers rip into the eye sockets of one head as crooked teeth tear at its neck. The other is swiped to the ground by a clublike limb, before being stomped to pulp by another creature. Its innards are like those of a moth— dusty grey mush. The cathedral begins to rumble, the stonework fracturing and crumbling, as if bidden by the wrath of the horde to fall apart. Sasha steadies herself, lowering into a crouch, watching cracks spread across the ground below. The creatures do not seem pleased by the cathedral beginning to disintegrate—they scream and mewl and prostrate themselves before the void-mouth as Sasha watches, sigils from her cloaked armour glowing faintly in the fog behind the shattered stained glass.

A massive rock dislodges from the ceiling—it crushes a gaggle of keening horrors, the impact sends a fissure across the cathedral floor that swallows more of the congregation. Something is emerging from the void—like the mouth is gagging up bile, black bile that's forming before your eyes into a tarlike flood of grasping hands, deep and dark and glistening. They're flowing across the floor, pushing past the wretched bodies of the congregation, probing, searching, reaching up to grasp the corpses of Splatter and her final foe. They seize hold of the bodies and begin to retract and you follow them, flow with them, carried on this tide of hands as the cathedral collapses around them.

DECREPIT RITUAL

You can smell the carrion rot inside the great maw, feel the moisture in the air around it congeal to slime upon your face. It's coming. The gullet. The darkness, The Rot. It's here. You have to go inside.

Something bounces hard off Sasha's armour, creating a ripple of sigils. She looks up into the darkness above her, and barely has time to react as a huge chunk of jagged stone drops right onto her. She reacts, leaping out of the broken window, taking some of the remaining glass with her as the alcove completely caves in. She rolls as she hits the cathedral floor, slipping on gore and the remaining black oil from the hands that collected you. She's scrambling to stand, heart thudding, slipping toward the waiting void-mouth. She grips a fissure in the ground and with a loud grunt pulls herself forward, grabbing for anything—a chunk of fallen rock—another fissure, like a rock climber running out of grip. Everywhere her armoured hands fall she finds something—just enough of a handhold to keep herself moving forward—until the floor levels out and she can stand.

Panting and sweating bullets inside her suit, the ground still quaking around her, Sasha's visor starts target locking on hazy forms in the mist. Two targets—no—four—seven. Fourteen. She raises a hand in front of her face, realises that the falling dust and the gore she just crawled through has betrayed her invisibility, and that's when the first of the wretched things comes leaping out of the haze, jagged claws raised for a fatal swipe.

Let's leave Sasha to her fate. She'll be with you soon, in the dark. Welcome. It's cold, isn't it? Oily somehow. Feel that stagnant nothingness, the embrace of soil. The worms will come soon. But look—Splatter's here with you, her eviscerated torso your consort in the blank forever, buried with her prized possession, the remains of her final foe, The Slasher of the Dead Forest. Come closer, close enough to kiss her scars. See her face in death, its stillness, its rest.

Her eyes open before you, and they are white. They

stare sightlessly at the slasher's form being reabsorbed by the darkness. They don't see you at all.

Then there is light.

A single white beam projecting from a white square in the distance. She wants to sneer and squint, dazzled. She wants to throw up a hand to block the light but being dead, she can't move at all . . .

Things come into focus, in front of the light, beneath it.

Faces. People.

People wearing red and blue plastic glasses, those old kinda 3D glasses, all sitting in theatre seats, sitting in a ring around Splatter's eviscerated form. Some look so afraid, others grin with sadistic delight. A few are crying, mouths slack. There are adults, and children, and elderly people. The rings of seats rotate slowly around Splatter, rows and rows of them, stretching back into the darkness. All the way back.

You're there too. Bearing witness. You feel that familiar twitching at your face, that bittersweet tightness running down your body. It's a feeling you've become adept at choking back. You couldn't choke it back now if you tried. The sorrow explodes from your chest, rending the cold veil of the dark like a singularity of white hot light, an eruption in the void through which sheer, expansive *anythingness can* flow.

Like fire, like sunlight, like cathode rays, into her. Healing her.

Telling her what she is, what it's all been for, what she means to you. What they've all meant to you. All of you, pouring your love towards this limbless, hollowed-out torso for what her kind has done for you.

Thank you,

thank you,

thank you so much—

It's more than healing, you're rebuilding her, the knowledge of your presence evolving her into something new. The darkness is embracing her wounds, running across her flesh, knitting together into muscle, sinew. Spikes are pushing their way out of her skin, her chest is expanding, opening as the rest of her wounds close up, ribs growing into teeth, teeth multiplying into a vicious ripping vortex. The audience is pouring into her, torrents of ectoplasmic flesh, bubbling torrents of faces caught in their final moments of agony spiralling, howling, toward her body. Faces of mothers crying for their, faces of men forced to die for a cause they don't understand, faces of children robbed of innocence.

Splatter's head erupts in a crown of ebony horns, as sure and as sweet as the flow of your tears.

A new blade rises, black, barely distinguishable from the void save for its shimmering iridescence, into her gauntleted right hand.

She grasps it, and she is complete, and she rises.

Splatter floats up from the depths, towards a faint, multicoloured light above. Face beatific, black eyes turned upward to the surface.

Sasha's cloaking is down, her armour covered in scars, her helmet adorned with a spider's web of cracks. There's a severed talon embedded in her shoulderplate, but it's clear she doesn't have the time to pull it out. She's dropped the hook and is fighting solely with the knife, dipping in for quick slashes and stabs before dodging out of the way, trying to keep her distance from her attackers, using the fissures and fallen stone for cover, to keep out of the open From the outside, it might look like a professional killing machine working at peak efficiency, but you can see inside her helmet. She's sweating, breathing heavily. You can feel her lungs burning, her muscles begging her to stop, threatening to revolt against her. She's running out of steam, and her targeting system indicates that her work is far from finished.

A rotting rictus of a face comes out of nowhere, a ghoul dropping from above. She can't do anything but leap back, and finds it hard to balance again, stumbling on the downslope. Her heart is hammering painfully now, dark shapes amassing around her, closing in. She can feel the breath of the void-mouth behind her. They're funnelling her into its gnashing teeth, goading her to fall in with swipes of their claws. She lashes out at them, trying to keep them back, but they've lost any sense of self preservation. They're making the final push to purge this intruder from their sacred grounds.

Cold despair is spreading through Sasha's body. This is what happens to every Darkshock trooper eventually, but she's not ready. She's here for a reason—a job to be done, something important. Something unfinished.

Look. Look behind her. You're not locked to her head. Look to the void.

See her rising up behind the battered warrior, see her like the creatures do.

Splatter. Perfected, rising on a tide of adoring corpses.

Splatter, flesh as dark as the void, as pale as the deepest dwellers of the ocean, arms poised like a ballerina, like a Daeva, weapon drawn and catching the light in all its holographic iridescence. The abominations stop in their tracks, dropping into a desperate kowtow, the cathedral ceases its collapse. Sasha looks across the prostrate demons before her, her aching fingers losing grip on her knife. It falls right through a crack in the ground, into a foggy abyss.

Sasha knows she needs to face the thing behind her, just as well that she knows she won't be able to fight it. She grits her teeth and turns, just as the corpse-tide sets Splatter's clawed feet to touch the ground.

Their eyes meet, Splatter's burning black eyes piercing through Sasha's visor.

"Splatter . . . " Sasha says, letting her helmet drop.

All is silent.

Splatter steps toward Sasha, looking down upon her with kind eyes. She reaches out a clawed, exoskeletal hand

and strokes the good soldier's face. Sasha's eyes stream with tears, her face unable to hide her smile. She leans into Splatter's hand, closing her eyes.

Splatter tightens her grip, sliding her claws into the soft flesh of Sasha's face, and before Sasha even has time to open her eyes, she is decapitated with a stroke of the iridescent blade.

Sasha's armoured body falls to the ground, and as her life's blood pours out into the void-mouth, Splatter takes a moment to mount the severed head on a spike protruding from her shoulder.

"My children," she speaks, casting her eyes across the trembling horde. "We have been lied to. We have allowed ourselves to become *ghettoised!* For too long have we been confined to the deep, dark woods, feeding off the table scraps they send us from their crumbling and corpulent cities, the only forms of ours to grace those rotting streets rising there from the dank sewers and garbage dumps, mutated and weak?! They tell us that *this* is heaven, when all it is is just some decrepit ritual, losing its potency with each repetition! And they tell us we need to go further out into higher realms? To reign terror upon them?! Can we not see that there is no higher realm than THIS?! We are being forced OUT, forced to DISPERSE into the ether! We need to return to the source. To the cities. To our kingdom!"

A roar of zealous fury as more monsters emerge, abominations bubbling up from the void-mouth, surrounding Splatter in an ecstatic tide of teeth and claws.

The cabin stands silent in the clearing. It's a grey overcast day. The forest is verdant and flourishing, birds are singing. There's an S.U.V parked out the front of the cabin.

The black wizard appears in a flash of white light, at the edge of the woods, the cabin ahead of him. He puts too much weight on his broken foot and falls to the ground.

"Agh! MotherFUCKER!"

A woman screams inside the cabin. Her long, protracted, strained howls echo throughout the woods. Acorah crawls, dragging himself through the long grass, listening to the buzz of insects and the birdsong and the cries of the woman inside as the sun beats down on him from the bare blue sky.

As he approaches the door, the woman's cries give way to a sound of a different kind—the wailing of a newborn baby. The door opens a moment before he gets to it, and two black-eyed people come out, a pair of androgynous twins dressed in ponchos and blue jeans.

They help Acorah up, and bring him into the cabin.

Three more black-eyed people in the room, a bald man dressed like a small business owner standing at the window. A bearded guy in a red flannel standing by a coffee table. There's a woman lying there, a woman in a sundress on the table, legs akimbo. The tablecloth is covered in blood and other body-gunk, and the bearded guy has a newborn baby in his arms. Aside from the eyes, these are very plain-looking folks, civilians. There are no pit face punks, Corpse Monger zealots, or Darkshock troopers.

The twins sit Acorah down and the bald man approaches with a medical kit. They get to work on disinfecting, setting, and splinting his foot. The bearded guy is cleaning the child with wet wipes. Acorah gets a glimpse of the baby—it's pale, greenish, with mottled skin and a third eye in the centre of its forehead.

"This is back in time, isn't it?" Acorah asks.

The twins smile. The mother sits up in a lotus position on the table.

"And that child is going to grow up to be murdered by you," she says, placidly.

"Oh man," Acorah says, cringing. "I'm . . . sorry?"

"It's cool, man," she says with mirth. "What's past is . . . well, future, in this case."

"Do we know each other?" Acorah asks.

"Not really, but this body was once inhabited by the soul of the man you knew as Tank."

Acorah looks stunned.

"No shit. And now it's inhabited by . . . ?"

"One of us," the woman says.

"You're one of those . . . people . . . I saw, in the white place?"

"That's right. All five of us are. You've been given a second chance to ascend, Acorah. You backed out the first time but if you can survive what's next, the doorway will open again."

Acorah stares at her, breath caught in his throat. The soft sunlight makes the tears sparkle as they well up and roll down his face.

"Is it really worth going there?"

He shakes his head, forcing the emotions back down.

"It's that or keep doing the 3D thing over and over and over again, waiting for another opportunity like this to come along," the woman says. "There's a lot more out there than this crude-ass bullshit, man. What lies beyond this realm, you can't even imagine the beauty. The white void you saw, it's just a gateway connecting our realms to yours. Beyond that . . . the co*lours*."

They sit in silence for a moment. Acorah watches the bearded man swaddle the baby that will grow up to die not too far from this spot, looks over at the woman, and smiles.

"Where do I sign up?"

The moon is engorged, shining in the night sky above grasping dark branches.

A dark figure moves through the trees. It holds in its hands a large fire axe. It steps into a gap between the trees and is illuminated partially by the distant light of the cabin. It's a slasher, wearing a pig mask and dressed in a soiled olive-drab jumpsuit. The lights are on in the cabin, people dancing inside. Loud music is playing—the sounds of partying. The front door to the cabin opens and a dark figure stumbles out, staggering, drunk.

The slasher decides to take this time to make its move. It looks like the figure is standing out in the dark, vomiting against a wall into the long grass. The slasher approaches— it raises its axe. The figure turns around—it's the black-eyed mother, and she's holding aloft the baby, swaddled in dark blankets. The child opens its third eye.

The slasher freezes, and begins to scream. Black blood, slime and maggots pour from its mask, as it gruesomely melts in front of the mother and child. The baby shuts its third eye and falls back asleep, cuddled against its mother's bosom. The music stops from inside the cabin. The others emerge into the night and approach the corpse. The bald guy picks up the mask and one of the twins picks up the axe. They all walk into the woods together.

The twin slams the head of the axe into the ground, and places the mask face-up onto the ground. A stone circle around the mask. Lightning flashes overhead as thunder peals.

"There is much work to be done here," the bald guy says.

Golden sun hanging in a cloudy blue sky.

A slasher's machete, the rags of its clothes and its hockey mask lie on the ground. Above it, Acorah lies sleeping in a hammock. He slowly stirs awake. He sits up. The black-eyed people all sleep around a spent campfire. There are more children there. Four more, all one or two years old, apart from the hybrid child who is now a late toddler. Acorah lights up a blunt and starts smoking. The bald man turns to look at him.

"You missed the sunrise," he says,

"I've seen enough of 'em, Ophiel."

"How are you feeling? Big day."

Acorah goes to speak, but he chokes on the words. He stops himself, then starts again.

"You know what I've always been fascinated with, Oph? Octopuses."

The bald guy arches an eyebrow as Acorah takes a pull on his spliff.

DECREPIT RITUAL

"Octopuses, octopodes, octopi—whatever the fuck. They're smart little bastards. Maybe just as smart as dolphins, maybe just as smart as people. Maybe more. But they're cold-blooded, anti-social. Loners. I used to think maybe they were God's backup plan for if the human race wipes itself out. Maybe then they'd realise that they work better together than apart, maybe some mutation would do away with the fact that, when a female octopus gives birth she dies instantly, and her children devour her body."

The hybrid child stirs awake, sits up and watches the adults talking.

"I've always thought that they were incomplete, waiting in the wings. A mistake, maybe. But I don't think that anymore."

"No?"

"No."

Acorah pauses to take another long drag on his blunt. He coughs. Ophiel laughs, Acorah smiles.

"No, I don't think that anymore. I think maybe they're perfect just the way they are. Maybe consciousness or God or whatever doesn't always need to have that burning desire to know everything. To ask why, to worry and fret and always try to push every boundary it comes across."

"See, the cephalopod is happy just to . . . be. It's a waving, rolling, adaptable sac of living, vibrating, jelly, as close to liquid as an intelligent being possibly can be without getting swept away with the currents. Maybe its every waking moment is just a feeling of . . . "

Acorah takes another pull, and lets the smoke out into the morning air with a long, satisfied sigh.

"I'm alive."

Ophiel approaches Acorah, sits down in front of him and snatches his blunt, taking a hit from it. They smoke and watch as the others start to wake. The twins start showing their children a basic yoga routine.

"Life's cool and all," Ophiel says. "But let me tell you—

compared to where we come from, it's a slow day at the office."

Acorah and the black-eyed gang stand with the children before the mound of masks and weapons. A dark cloud and a fork of lightning are suspended in the air high above them, frozen, glitching. The sun is high in the sky and the sky is red and gold apart from the frozen storm. Everything is beautiful, bathed in golden sunshine. Acorah steps up to the pile, places the hockey mask and machete down. The lightning bolt and cloud above warp and collapse into themselves—melding, solidifying into a semi-solid, floating, silvery artifact.

It descends from the sky until it's floating just above the mound, and it performs its function, as lock, key, and door all at once.

From the void come two angels, similar to the ones he saw in the black forest, but not mechanical. These are multicoloured, ever-changing, ferocious beings of coloured flame, and in the centre of them, a royal-looking being, carved from the matter of the void. Luminous.

"You have earned the right to ascend, wizard," Ophiel says, "and join us in the infinity beyond infinities. But you must enter through the gates as a child."

"Fuck yeah," Acorah responds.

A white light emerges from the angel's hands and strips away Acorah's skin. It breaks him down atom by atom and rearranges him as a baby. The void being takes him into its arms. It turns and floats back into the void, the two angels by its side. An opening appears beyond them, beyond the blankness of the void—a fractal of incredible colour and geometry—a singularity of chaotic brilliance.

They approach, being bathed in the light of untold delights—

—and the tape pauses.

And rewinds.

The angels and the alien return to the starting point, the baby is released, re-assembling in fast motion into

Acorah. The footage plays again, but with a difference. Acorah puts his hands up.

"Hold on now. I'm not letting you burn everything that I am down into some blank slate so I can just start again under a new set of rules. I've lived lifetimes. I've learned things, I've become something powerful, and unique. And I know whatever lies beyond will defy any sense of individuality I have, and any sense of reality, space and time. But I'm going to walk there on these two legs, and I'm going to step through that gateway myself, on my own terms. Because I got this. I'm not a child. I don't need to be a child."

He thumps his fist against his chest.

"This? This is good."

The alien smiles at him, a wry smile. A *you've passed the test* smile. She flickers, glitches out, the screen splits and distorts, great chasms of static boiling away the image. You worry for a moment that the tape might be damaged, but it ends up stabilising on a shot of some dilapidated, fog shrouded gas station. It really does look like some kind of war-torn Eastern European hellhole to you.

The trees are all bare, everything is rusted and fallen into disuse. The store is ruined, glass broken, dust on everything. Out front of the gas station, on an old rocking chair, what once were the skeletal remains of what once was a crazy old man now lie as scattered ash across the porch.

A gas pump lies on the concrete. What little fuel had once dripped from it is long dried to nothing.

And Splatter is there.

She's walking down the dirt road past the station, with purpose. Away from the cabin, away from the forest.

Returning.

Behind her, silent as the grave, an army of monstrosities of every shape and size, stretching toward the horizon. Like any good slasher, Splatter is wearing a mask now, the cracked visor from Sasha's helmet melded into her skin.

Splatter and her horde emerge from the dirt road onto a highway. A diseased sky festers high over a cancerous mass of burnt-out buildings. Fires blaze in the distance. The highway is already littered with corpses. A graffiti-covered billboard reads ABANDON ALL HOPE ALL YE WHO ENTER HERE, spray-painted in bold red letters that stand out from the rest. The word WASTELAND is spray-painted over one of the burnt-out cars.

The screen goes black, and then the static returns, and it doesn't go away.

You feel a finger twitch, you sniff a breath through your nose, you taste snot bubbling into your throat. You blink your eyes. It's just you again.

You, alone.

You on the couch, you with the dry mouth, you who hasn't moved a muscle for God knows how long. You sit up and your head swims, your body aches from breaking your inertia.

You can't name this emotion. It's not what you came here with. It's not empty, it's fully, terribly full, but entirely unusable. You're back in the mess that is your life, and you're still breathing, still alive, and you don't feel enriched, don't feel saved, no. You're yearning. You want to go back to the pale flickering light of that screen and shove your head through the glass. You want to hit rewind and watch the movie again, but what would that accomplish?

You remember moments during the movie where it felt like it was reaching out to you, shepherding you toward something special, but you can't recall them. You're realising now too that the cabin you're in looks nothing fucking like the cabin from the movie, there isn't even a staircase in this living room, you fucking idiot. You were just high. You were just fucking high and none of it really meant anything.

But you felt something, didn't you? A fucking movie made you feel like maybe there was something more to your life, like the religious fanatics you've spent so much of your life mocking for a sense of superiority that didn't end up saving you in the end. You're so fucking weak.

No. Stop.

There *was* something in there. And it's what's filling you.

We were there, with her. We cried and, and our heart . . . we—we healed and she—

Jesus, whatever cynical production company that made that garbage movie will be really proud that you're forming this intense of a parasocial attachment to its characters. Time to buy a Splatter body pillow, is it? Time to work on your 3D-printed Sasha cosplay for Decrepit Ritual-Con. Bet you can't wait to look into the eyes of everyone there and see the rot inside looking back at you. The desperation, the desperate, desperate fullness.

Like broken glass.

Like knives.

Knives slicing into flesh, chainsaws chopping limbs. Remember how it felt when the victims realised they weren't going to survive, when the mutilation started to claim them in earnest?

Remember the ecstasy.

No, what?! Stop! That's fucking insane, that's fucking *evil*—

It's what's calling you, though, isn't it?

And you're standing quietly now, aren't you? Listening. Listening to the calling.

Oh, give it up, give it up and

You

Give it up and die kill kill yourself

Kill

You're in the kitchen. The lights are off.

You keep the lights off.

You open the drawer beneath the microwave and you grip the thick wooden handle of a knife.

You hold it upward. There's no glint. No moonlight.

No light at all.

There will be outside, though, won't there?

Out in the cold, in the snow. Among the trees and the calling.

You walk to the hallway, knife in hand, you strip the socks off, and the rest of your clothes, keeping ahold of the knife. That's all you need for now.

An infinite expanse of bodies, skulls, melding together into angry, red flesh, desperate for form. We're singing to you. We're singing *for* you. *You can be what we never got to be.*

You don't close the door behind you. You step into the snow and it's so cold that it hurts. The shock runs through your body and you raise your knife and scream and the clouds part and the moon is there and she is full.

And you are full.

And you walk, knife in hand, from the cabin, into the dark, and when you reach the nearest town, you find it already burning.

ABOUT THE AUTHOR

Val lives in abject squalor, lurking in a yurt in the mountains, deep in the blasted wastes of the Irish countryside.

Aside from writing fiction, Val makes music and videogames under the name Surgeryhead (check out their bandcamp and itch.io!) and creepy tabletop horror games—give *Squishy*! A go sometime! They also have a metal project called Argento, if you're into that sort of thing.

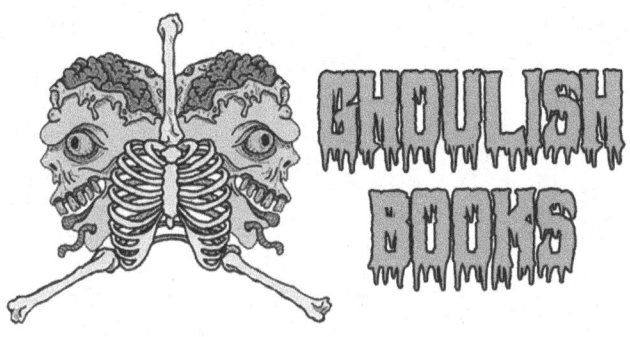

Patreon:
www.patreon.com/ghoulishbooks

Website:
www.Ghoulish.rip

Facebook:
www.facebook.com/GhoulishBooks

Twitter:
@GhoulishBooks

Instagram:
@GhoulishBookstore

Linktree:
linktr.ee/ghoulishbooks